"Duvernay is where my son belongs."

Tabby's gaze collided with the cold glitter of Christien's challenging appraisal. "At present, our son belongs with me—"

"Long may that arrangement last," Christien remarked softly. "Children need their mothers as much as they need their fathers."

"Thank you for that vote of confidence." Tabby tilted her chin, but her heart was starting to thump very fast. "Although I have to admit that I haven't a clue why you should take the trouble to tell me that."

"I'm prepared to be generous and make you an offer—"

"I'm not very fussed about the kind of offer you make," Tabby declared with complete truth.

"Either you hear me out or my lawyers deal with this situation. Your choice," Christien replied, as smooth as silk.

"We don't have a situation here. I was the one who told you that Jake was your son and you can see him as often as you like...."

"I want Jake and you to live with me."

Lynne Graham

THE FRENCHMAN'S LOVE–CHILD

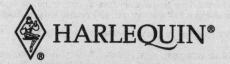

TORONTO • NEW YORK • LONDON
AMSTERDAM • PARIS • SYDNEY • HAMBURG
STOCKHOLM • ATHENS • TOKYO • MILAN • MADRID
PRAGUE • WARSAW • BUDAPEST • AUCKLAND

ISBN 0-373-12355-8

THE FRENCHMAN'S LOVE-CHILD

First North American Publication 2003.

Copyright © 2003 by Lynne Graham.

All rights reserved. Except for use in any review, the reproduction or utilization of this work in whole or in part in any form by any electronic, mechanical or other means, now known or hereafter invented, including xerography, photocopying and recording, or in any information storage or retrieval system, is forbidden without the written permission of the publisher, Harlequin Enterprises Limited, 225 Duncan Mill Road, Don Mills, Ontario, Canada M3B 3K9.

All characters in this book have no existence outside the imagination of the author and have no relation whatsoever to anyone bearing the same name or names. They are not even distantly inspired by any individual known or unknown to the author, and all incidents are pure invention.

This edition published by arrangement with Harlequin Books S.A.

® and TM are trademarks of the publisher. Trademarks indicated with ® are registered in the United States Patent and Trademark Office, the Canadian Trade Marks Office and in other countries.

Visit us at www.eHarlequin.com

Printed in U.S.A.

CHAPTER ONE

A QUESTIONING frown in his keen dark eyes, Christien Laroche studied the portrait of his late great-aunt, Solange. A quiet woman who had never made a wave in her life, Solange had nonetheless startled her entire family with the contents of her will.

'Extraordinary!' a cousin commented with fierce disapproval. 'What could Solange have been thinking of?'

'It grieves me to say it but my poor sister's mind must have weakened towards the end,' an aghast brother of the deceased lamented.

'*Vraiment!* To leave a piece of the Duvernay estate away from her own family and favour a foreigner instead...it is unbelievable!' another exclaimed in outrage.

In a more laid-back mood, Christien would have been struggling not to laugh at the genuine horror that his relatives were exhibiting. Wealth had not lessened their passionate attachment to the family estate for that atavistic link back to the very land itself still ran deep and strong in every French soul. But they *were* all over-reacting for the bequest was tiny in terms of monetary worth. The Duvernay estate ran to many thousands of acres and the property in question was a little cottage on a mere patch of ground. Even so, Christien had also been angered by a bequest that he considered both regrettable and highly inappropriate. Why had his great-aunt left anything at all to a young woman she had only met a few times several years earlier? That was

the biggest mystery and one he would have given much
to comprehend.

'Indeed, Solange must have been very ill for her will
is a terrible insult to my feelings,' his widowed mother,
Matilde, complained tearfully. 'That girl's father mur-
dered my husband, yet my own aunt has rewarded her!'

Lean, strong face grim at the speed with which his
parent had made that unfortunate connection, Christien
remained by the elegant windows that overlooked
Duvernay's glorious gardens while the lady who acted
as his mother's companion comforted the weeping
older woman. Although almost four years had passed
since his father's death, Matilde Laroche still lived behind lowered blinds in her huge Paris apartment, wore
the dark colours of mourning and rarely went out or
entertained. Christien was now challenged to recall that
his mother had once been an outgoing personality with
a warm sense of humour. Indeed in the radius of her
unending grief he felt helpless for neither counselling
nor medication had managed to alleviate her suffering
to any appreciable degree.

At the same time, it was only fair to acknowledge
that Matilde Laroche *had* suffered a devastating loss.
His parents had been childhood sweethearts and life-
long best friends and their marriage had been one of
unusual intimacy. Furthermore, his father had only
been fifty-four when he died. A prominent banker,
Henri Laroche had rejoiced in the vigour and health of
a man in the very prime of life. However, that had not
protected Christien's father from a cruelly premature
and pointless death at the hands of a drunk driver.

That drunken driver had been Tabitha Burnside's
father, Gerry. In all, five families had been shattered
that appalling night by just *one* car accident and Henri

Laroche had not been the only casualty. Gerry Burnside had also managed to kill himself, four of his passengers and leave a fifth seriously injured, who later died.

That fatal summer, four English families had been sharing the rambling farmhouse situated just down the hill from the imposing Laroche vacation home in the Dordogne. His late father had remarked that he should have bought the property himself to prevent it being occupied throughout the season by a horde of noisy holiday-makers. Naturally no Laroche would have dreamt of mixing with tourists, whose sole idea of amusement seemed to rest on getting sunburnt, drunk and eating too much. However, his parents had only stayed at their villa on a couple of occasions that summer and most weeks, aside of visits from his friends and initially from his lover at the time, Christien had been left in peace to work.

There had been three Burnsides in the large party staying at the farmhouse: Gerry Burnside, his youthful second wife, Lisa, and his daughter from his first marriage, Tabby. Before Christien had met Tabby, he had only ever seen the two young women at a distance and would not have been able to distinguish one from the other. Both Lisa and Tabby had been shapely blondes and, not only had he initially assumed that they were sisters he had also assumed that they were of a similar age. He had had no idea whatsoever that *one* of them had been still only a schoolgirl…

Of course, even at a distance, Tabby had had promiscuous tramp written all over her, Christien conceded wryly, his wide sensual mouth curling with disdain. Like most young males in the grip of rampant lust, however, he had still been an eager participant in all that had followed. Tabby's nude nightly swimming sessions in the *gîte*'s underwater-lit pool could only have been staged for his benefit. He would not have stayed home specially to watch her, but, on the evenings that he had enjoyed a glass of wine on the villa terrace, her provocative displays of her full breasts and deliciously curved bottom had provided him with considerable entertainment.

He didn't blame himself for enjoying the view. Any guy would have got hot and hard watching her flaunt her charms. Any guy would have decided that, at the first opportunity, he would take immediate advantage of so obvious an invitation. Of course, it had not occurred to Christien then to wonder why Tabby so often stayed at home while the rest of the party dined out every evening. Only with hindsight had he appreciated that she must have been targeting him all along. Of course, she had first seen him in the village and would soon have found out who he was and, perhaps more crucially, what he was worth. Realising that the Laroche villa overlooked the pool at the farmhouse, she had guessed that sooner or later he was certain to catch a glimpse of her bathing naked.

That from the outset Tabby should have set out to entrap him surprised Christien not at all. Even as a teenager, he had learnt that women found his sleek, dark good looks irresistible and were capable of going to extraordinary lengths to attract his attention. But he had never been vain about his phenomenal success with the female sex. He was well aware that sex and money together provided a powerful draw. He had been born very, very rich. He was an only child, born to two wealthy only children and, as an adult, he had become even richer.

Blessed with the Laroche talent for making money

and sensational entrepreneurial skills, Christien had dropped out of university at the age of twenty. Within nine months, he had made his first million in business. Five years on from there, sole owner of an international airline that was breaking all profit records, and suffering from a certain amount of burn-out from working a seven-day week, Christien had been getting bored. That summer, he had been ripe for something a little different and Tabby had more than satisfied him in that department.

Tabby had played no games and she had come to him on his terms. He had had her on the first date. Six weeks of the wildest sex he had ever experienced had followed. He had been obsessed with her. Her strange insistence on not staying the night in his bed and keeping their entanglement a secret from her family and their friends had added an illicit thrill to their every encounter. What he would never, ever forget, however, was that after only six weeks of explosive sexual fulfilment he had been ready to propose marriage so that he could have access to that fabulous body of hers at all hours of the day.

Marriage! Christien still shuddered at that degrading recollection. His meteoric IQ rating had not done him much good while the urge to indulge his powerful libido had overruled every other restraint. The shattering discovery that he had been making love to a schoolgirl had blown him away. A schoolgirl of seventeen, who was a compulsive liar!

While Veronique had been agonising over how best he might protect himself from the threat of a horrendous scandal, Christien had still been so lost in lust that he had decided that he could cope with a teenage wife whom he would teach to tell the truth and keep in bed most of the time anyway. But, the next day, he had seen his potential child bride behaving like a slut with a spotty youth on a motorbike and, all rage, disbelief and disgust aside, he had immediately broken free of his obsession...

'If that Burnside girl sets foot on Laroche soil, it will dishonour your father's memory!' Matilde Laroche protested.

Drawn from his brooding recollections with a vengeance, Christien almost winced at the tearful note in his mother's overwrought exclamation. 'There is no question of that happening,' he asserted with soothing conviction. 'She will receive an offer to sell the property back to the estate and she will naturally accept the money.'

'This matter is so unpleasant for you to deal with,' Veronique remarked in a sympathetic and discreet murmur at his side. 'Allow me to take care of it for you.'

'As always you are generous, but in this case there is no need.' Christien surveyed the beautiful, elegant brunette he planned to marry with open appreciation.

Veronique Giraud was everything a Laroche wife should be. He had known her all his life and their backgrounds were similar. A corporate lawyer, she was an excellent hostess as well as being tolerant of her future mother-in-law's emotional fragility. But neither love nor lust featured in Christien's relationship with his fiancée. Both of them considered mutual respect and honesty of greater importance. Although Veronique was naturally willing to give him children, she had little enthusiasm for physical intimacy and had already made it clear that she would prefer him to satisfy his needs with a mistress.

Christien was quite content with that arrangement.

Indeed the knowledge that even marriage would not deprive him of that valuable male freedom to essentially do as he liked, when he liked, had very much increased his willingness to embrace the matrimonial bond.

In little more than a month, he would be over in London on business. He would pay Tabby Burnside a visit and offer to buy the cottage back from her. No doubt she would feel flattered by his personal attention. He wondered what she looked like some years on... faded? At only twenty-one? He almost shrugged. What did it matter to him? But he also smiled.

A house in France, Tabby reflected dreamily, a place of their own in the sun...

'Of course, you'll sell the old lady's cottage for the best price you can get,' Alison Davies assumed on her niece's behalf. 'It'll fetch a healthy sum.'

Fresh, clean country air in exchange for the city traffic fumes that she was convinced had made her toddler son prone to asthma, Tabby thought happily.

'You and Jake will have something to put away for a rainy day.' Her aunt, a slender brunette with sensible grey eyes, nodded with approval at that idea.

Lost in her own thoughts, Tabby was still mulling over the extraordinary fact that Solange Roussel had left her a French property. It was fate, it *had* to be. Of that latter reality, Tabby was convinced. Her son had French blood in his veins and now, by an immense stroke of good fortune and when she least expected it, she had inherited a home for them both on French soil. Of course that was meant to be! Who could possibly doubt it? She looked into the small back garden where Jake was playing. He was an enchanting child with mischievous brown eyes, skin with a warm olive tone and a shock of silky dark curls. His asthma was only mild at present, but who could say how much worse it might get if they remained in London?

The same day that the letter from the French *notaire* had arrived to inform her of her inheritance, Tabby had begun planning a new life for herself and her child in France. After all, the timing could not have been more perfect: Tabby had been desperate to come up with an acceptable excuse for moving out of her aunt's comfortable town house. Alison Davies was only ten years older than her niece. When, in the wake of her father's death, Tabby had been left penniless and pregnant into the bargain, Alison had offered her niece a home. Tabby was very aware of how great a debt of gratitude she owed to the other woman.

But, just a week earlier, Tabby had overheard a heated exchange between Alison and her boyfriend, Edward, which had left her squirming with guilty discomfiture. Edward was going to take a year out from work to travel. Tabby had already known that and she had also been aware that her aunt had decided not to accompany him. What Tabby had not realised, until she accidentally heard the couple arguing, was that Alison Davies might be denying herself her heart's desire sooner than ask her niece to find somewhere else to live.

'You don't need to use up your precious savings! Thanks to your parents you own this house and you could rent it out for a small fortune while we were abroad. That would cover *all* your expenses,' Edward had been pointing out forcefully in the kitchen when Tabby, having returned from her evening job, had been fumbling for her key outside the back door.

'We've been over this before,' Alison had been protesting unhappily. 'I just *can't* ask Tabby to move out so that I can offer this place to strangers. She can't afford decent accommodation—'

'And whose fault is that? She got pregnant at seventeen and now she's paying for her foolish mistake!' Edward had slammed back angrily. 'Does that mean *we* have to pay for it too? Isn't it bad enough that we're rarely alone together and that when we are you're always babysitting her kid?'

Tabby was still terribly hurt and mortified by the memory of that biting censure. But she regarded it as justifiable criticism. She felt that she ought to have seen for herself that she had overstayed her welcome in her aunt's home. She was appalled that Alison should have been prepared to make such a sacrifice on her behalf, for her aunt had already been very generous to her. Indeed, all that Tabby could now think about was moving out as soon as was humanly possible. Only then would Alison feel free to do as she liked with her own life and her own home. At the same time, however, she did not want the other woman to suspect that she might have overheard that revealing dialogue.

'I'm afraid I *still* can't stop wondering why some elderly French lady should have remembered you in her will,' Alison Davies confided with a bemused shake of her head.

Dragged out of her own preoccupied thoughts by the raising of that topic yet again, Tabby screened her expressive green eyes and looped a stray strand of caramel-blonde hair back behind one small ear. Some things were too personal and private to share even with her aunt. 'Solange and I got on very well—'

'But you only met a couple of times...'

'You've got to remember that what she's left me can only be a tiny part of what she owned because she was very well off,' Tabby muttered in an awkward attempt to explain. 'I'm over the moon that she's left me the cottage but I suppose in her eyes...it was just a little token.'

Tabby was reluctant to admit that, on each of the occasions she had met Solange Roussel, she had connected with the older woman on a very emotional level. The first time she had been bubbling with happiness and quite unafraid to admit that she adored Christien. The second time she had been a lot less sure of herself and she had not been able to hide her fear that Christien was losing interest...and the third and final time?

Months after that fatal French holiday that had torn apart so many lives, Tabby had travelled back to France alone to attend the accident enquiry. She had been desperate to see Christien again. She had believed that the passage of time would have eased his bitterness and helped him to acknowledge that they had *both* lost much-loved parents in that horrendous crash. However, she had soon learnt her mistake for, if anything, the intervening months had only made Christien colder and more derisive. Even Veronique, who had once been so friendly towards her, had become distant and hostile. As Gerry Burnside's daughter, Tabby had become a pariah to everyone who had lost a relative or been injured in any way by that car crash.

On the day of that enquiry Tabby had finally grown up and it had been almost as cruel and life-changing an ordeal for her as the aftermath of that car accident. Even though the previous months had been a nightmare struggle for Tabby to get through, and she had had to borrow money from her aunt just to make that trip back

to France, she had still been full of naive hopes and
dreams of how Christien would react to the news that
he was the father of her newborn baby boy.

But on the day of that official hearing, her dream
castles had crumbled into dust. In the end she had not
even got to tell Christien that she had given birth to
his son, for she had baulked at making that announcement in front of an audience and he had refused her
request for a moment's privacy in which to talk. Devastated by that merciless refusal to accord her even the
tiniest privilege in acknowledgement of their past intimacy, Tabby had fled outside sooner than break down
in tears in front of him, his relatives and friends. Out
there in the street a hand had closed over hers in a
comforting but shy gesture. In disconcertion, Tabby
had glanced up to meet the look of pained compassion
in Solange Roussel's understanding gaze.

'I'm sorry that the family should have come between
you and Christien,' the older woman had sighed with
sincere regret. 'It should not be that way.'

Before Tabby had been able to respond and admit
that she suspected something rather less presentable
than family loyalties might ultimately have led to her
having been dumped by Christien, Solange had hurried
back into the building where the enquiry was being
held. His great-aunt had doubtless been fearful of being
seen to show sympathy to the drunk driver's daughter.

'You are planning to sell this French property…
aren't you?' Alison pressed without warning.

Tabby drew in a deep breath in preparation for
breaking news that she knew would surprise the brunette. 'No…I'm hoping to keep it.'

Her aunt frowned. 'But the cottage is on Christien
Laroche's Brittany estate…isn't it?'

'Solange said that Christien rarely went to Duvernay because he much prefers the city to the country,' Tabby volunteered stiffly, for even voicing *his* name out loud was a challenge for her. 'She also told me that the estate was absolutely enormous and that her little place was right on the very edge of it. If I keep myself to myself, as I plan to do, he's not even going to know I'm there!'

Alison still looked troubled. 'Are you sure that you aren't secretly hoping to see him again?'

'Of course, I'm not!' Tabby grimaced in embarrassment. 'Why would I want to see him again?'

'To tell him about Jake?'

'I don't want to tell him about Jake now. The time for that has been and gone.' Tabby tilted up her chin for if Christien and his snobby, judgemental family had been affronted even by the sight of *her* at that accident enquiry, her son's very existence would surely only further offend and disgust them. 'Jake's mine and we're managing fine.'

Alison said nothing, for she was not convinced and she knew just how vulnerable Tabby could be with her open heart and trusting nature. She had always felt very protective towards her late sister's only child and she was well aware of the dangerous effect that her niece appeared to have on the opposite sex. Tabby had blonde hair the colour of streaky toffee, green eyes, dimples and an incredible figure that bore a close resemblance to an old-fashioned hourglass. The one quality that Tabby had in super-abundance was the sort of natural sex appeal that caused havoc.

When Tabby walked down the street, men were so busy craning their necks to get a better look at her luscious curves that they had been known to crash their cars. In actuality misfortune *did* seem to follow Tabby around, Alison conceded ruefully, thinking of the amount of bad luck that had shaped her niece's life in recent years. Yet, Tabby would still rush into situations where angels feared to tread and, even though the results were often disastrous, she remained an incurable optimist.

Reminding herself of that fact, Alison rested anxious grey eyes on the young woman seated opposite her. 'I hate to rain on your parade, *but*…I suspect you haven't considered how expensive it would be to maintain a holiday home in another country.'

'Oh, I'm not thinking of the cottage as a holiday home! My goodness, is that what you thought?' Tabby laughed out loud at the very idea. 'I'm talking about a permanent move…about Jake and I making a new life in France—'

Startled by that sudden announcement, her aunt stared at her. 'But you can't do that—'

'Why not? I can do my miniature work anywhere and sell what I make on the internet. I'm already building up a customer base and what could be more inspiring than the French landscape?' Tabby asked with sunny enthusiasm. 'I know that to start with things will be tight financially, but, because I own the cottage, I won't need much of an income to get by on. Jake's at the perfect age to move abroad and learn a second language as well—'

'For goodness' sake, you're making all these plans and you haven't even *seen* this cottage yet!' Alison exclaimed in reproof.

'I know.' Tabby grinned. 'But I'm planning to go over on the ferry next week to check it out.'

'What if it's uninhabitable?'

Tabby squared her slight shoulders. 'I'll deal with that when I see it.'

'I just don't think that you're being practical,' Alison Davies said more gently. 'Going to live abroad may seem like an exciting proposition, but you have Jake to consider. You'll have no support network to fall back on in France, nobody to help out if you need to work or you fall ill.'

'But I'm looking forward to being independent.'

At that declaration, her companion looked taken aback and then rather hurt.

Steeling herself to press home that point, Tabby swallowed hard for she knew it was the most convincing argument that she could put forward. 'I need to stand on my own feet, Alison…I'm twenty-one now.'

Her cheeks rather flushed, her aunt got up and began clearing away the supper dishes. 'I can understand that but I don't want you to burn your boats here and then find out too late that you've made an awful mistake.'

Tabby sat there and thought about all the mistakes she had made. Jake came running in the back door and ran full tilt into her arms. Breathless, laughing and smelling of fresh air and muddy little boy, he scrambled onto her knee and gave her a boisterous hug. 'I love you, Mum,' he said chirpily.

Her eyes stung and she held him tight. Most people were too polite or kind to say it, but she knew that they all thought Jake was her biggest mistake so far. Yet when Tabby's life had fallen apart only the prospect of the baby she'd carried had given her the strength to keep going and trust that the future would be happier. Christien had been like the sun in her world and it literally *had* felt like eternal darkness and gloom when he had gone from it again.

A frown still pleating her brows, Alison turned from the sink to study the younger woman again. 'Before you moved in here I worked with a guy called Sean Wendell,' she confided. 'He was mad about France and he moved to Brittany and set up an agency managing rental property. I still hear from Sean every Christmas. Why don't I phone him and ask him to give you some support while you're over there?'

As Tabby emerged from her preoccupation to give her aunt a look of surprise the brunette grimaced. 'I know, I *know*…I shouldn't be interfering but, for my sake, let Sean help out. If you don't, I'll be worrying myself sick about you!'

'But exactly what am I going to need support with?' Tabby enquired ruefully.

'Well, for a start you'll have to deal with the *notaire* and there's sure to be a few legalities to sort out. Your French is fairly basic and might not be up to the challenge.'

Tabby knew that her linguistic skills were rusty but was dismayed by the prospect of being saddled with a stranger. In truth, though, at that moment it was hard for Tabby to focus her mind on what was only a minor annoyance because the past had a far stronger hold on her thoughts. As she helped Jake get ready for bed, memories that were both painful and exhilarating were starting to drag her back almost four years in time to that summer that already seemed a lifetime ago…

For all of her childhood that she could remember, the Burnside family and their three closest friends—the Stevensons, the Rosses and the Tarberts—had gone to the Dordogne for their annual holiday and either rented *gîtes* very close to each other or found accommodation large enough to share. The Stevensons had

had a daughter called Pippa who was the same age as Tabby and her best friend. The Ross family had had two daughters, Hilary, who was six months younger and her kid sister, Emma and the Tarberts had had one daughter, Jen. Way back when Tabby, Pippa, Hilary and Jen had been toddlers, the girls had attended the same church playgroup and their mothers had become friendly. Even though their respective families had eventually moved to other locations and much had changed in all their lives, those friendships had endured and the vacations in France had continued.

But in the autumn of Tabby's sixteenth year, the contented family life that she had pretty much taken for granted had vanished without any warning whatsoever. Her mother had caught influenza and had died from a complication. Gerry Burnside had been devastated by his wife's sudden death but just six short months later, and without discussing his plans with anybody, he had remarried. His second wife, Lisa, had been the twenty-two-year-old blonde receptionist who had worked in his car sales showroom. Tabby had been as shattered by that startling development as everybody else had been.

Almost overnight her father had turned into an unfamiliar stranger, determined to dress like a much younger man and party and behave like one too. He had no longer had time to spare for his daughter, because his bride had not only been jealous of his attention but also prone to throwing screaming tantrums if she hadn't got it. To please Lisa, he had bought another house and spent a fortune on it. From the start, Lisa had resented Tabby and had made it clear that her stepdaughter had been an unwelcome third wheel.

Lisa had certainly not wanted to go on the traditional

French holiday with her husband's friends that summer, but for once Gerry Burnside had stood his ground. Full of resentment, Lisa had made no attempt to fit in and had gloried in shocking her besotted husband's friends with her behaviour. A helpless onlooker suffering from all the supersensitivity of a teenager, Tabby had died a thousand deaths of embarrassment and had avoided being in the adults' company as much as she'd been able.

At the same time, unfortunately, Tabby had also felt like a fish out of water with Pippa, Hilary and Jen. Her friends, with their stable homes and loving parents still safe and intact, had seemed aeons removed from her in their every innocence. In addition she had been too loyal to her father to tell anyone just how dreadfully unhappy and isolated she'd been feeling. And then she had seen Christien and all her own petty anxieties and the rest of the world, and indeed everyone in it, had no longer existed for her.

It had only been the second day of their vacation. Mulling over the humiliation of having been called a 'nasty little bitch' and sworn at by Lisa in front of Pippa's aghast parents at breakfast time, Tabby had been sitting on the wall under the plane trees in the sleepy little village below the farmhouse. A long, low yellow sports car had growled down the hill and round the corner like a snarling beast and had come to a throaty, purring halt a little further down the street.

A very tall, well-built male wearing sunglasses had climbed out and sauntered into the little pavement café. Clad in an off-white shirt with the cuffs carelessly turned back and beige chinos of faultless cut, he had sunk down at a table and tossed a note to the owner's son, who had run into the shop next door to fetch him a newspaper. He had been so cool she had been welded to his every move.

The bar owner had greeted him with pronounced respect and had polished his already clean table. The coffee and the ubiquitous croissant had been delivered with an understated flourish and a moment later the newspaper. The little scene had been *so* French she had been fascinated. Then Christien had hooked his sunglasses into the pocket of his shirt. She had found herself staring at that lean bronzed face, the black hair flopping over his brow, the stunning dark-as-midnight eyes that seemed to glint gold in the sunlight, and her heart had hammered so fast it had been quite impossible for her to breathe.

For a heartbeat in time, Christien had looked back at her and she had been mesmerised, entrapped, taken by storm. That one look had been all it had taken. *Un coup de foudre*, love like lightning striking fast and hard. He had turned his attention to his newspaper. She had feasted her eyes on him, quite content just to stare and admire and marvel at his lithe bronzed perfection. Eventually he had strolled back across the pavement and swung back into his equally beautiful car and driven off again…slowly, certainly slowly enough to get a good look at her from behind his tinted car windows.

'Who is he?' she had asked the sullen youth who cleaned the pool at the farmhouse.

He had not recognised her enraptured description of Christien, but he had recognised the car she had described. 'Christien Laroche…his family have a villa up the hill. He's richer than a bank.'

'Is he married?'

'You must be joking. He has a string of hot slick

chicks. Why? Do you fancy your chances? You'd only be a baby to a bigshot businessman like him!' he had mocked.

On that recollection Tabby forced her thoughts back into the present, but she was annoyed with herself for thinking about Christien. Solange's legacy had tempted her into looking back to events that had no relevance except insofar as they had taught her a few much-needed lessons. She tucked Christien's son into bed and smiled down at him with tender appreciation. Whether she liked it or not, even at three years old Jake was his father in miniature, for his looks and height were pure Laroche and he was much too clever for his own good. But, if Tabby had anything to do with it, Jake would never, ever regard women as numbers to be scored off on some sexual hit list.

The following week, Tabby sold the one valuable item that she still possessed: a diamond hair clip that Christien had once given her. It did not hurt to part with it as she had not worn it since the night he'd given it to her and she did not live a life where diamond hair clips were of any use. She was delighted to discover that the clip was worth a great deal more money than she had ever appreciated. Indeed, with careful handling the proceeds of the sale enabled her to buy an old van to use for transport and left her with enough cash to meet the other expenses entailed in moving across the English Channel. Alison had persuaded her to make her first trip to France alone and Tabby planned to leave her son in her aunt's care over a long weekend. The cottage was certain to need a good clean and clouds of dust would only leave poor Jake coughing and wheezing.

One week before her departure, Tabby had just got

back from taking Jake to nursery school and was in the midst of eating her breakfast when the doorbell sounded. A piece of toast in her hand, she went to answer the front door. When she had to tip her head back to get a proper look at the tall dark male in the charcoal-grey business suit poised on the step, her toast fell from her nerveless fingers.

'I would have phoned to tell you that I intended to call, but your aunt's number is unlisted,' Christien murmured, smooth as glass.

The breath feathered in Tabby's constricted throat. His fabulous accent purred down her spine like the tantalising promise of something dark and forbidden. Her senses snapped onto instant alert and she could not drag her bewildered gaze from his lean, dark, exotic features. Without even knowing she was doing it, she backed away, reacting to a subconscious feeling of being under threat. Exciting threat, though, delicious threat, the kind of threat that appealed to all that was weak and wanton in her nature. But he *was* even more irresistible than she remembered and, no matter how much she hated herself for it, her heart was already thumping like a road drill inside her.

Yet she could not really believe that Christien Laroche stood in front of her again, that he should be on the brink of entering Alison's home or that he should even deign to speak to her. How *could* that feel real?

Tabby trembled, dilated eyes green as emeralds pinned to him. At their last meeting, he had regarded her with a derisive distaste that had pierced her like a knife, and there might as well have been poison on that blade for the pain had not ended there. She had hated herself for loving him, loathed herself for the craving she could not suppress and despised her sorry self for striving to trace Christien's features in her son's innocent baby face.

'What are you doing here?' Tabby breathed shakily.

His brilliant dark eyes narrowed and a slight curve that only hinted at a smile softened the line of his wide, firm male mouth as he thrust the door shut in his wake. He dominated the space she was in and shrunk the hall of Alison's house to claustrophobic proportions. He was much taller, broader and more powerfully impressive than she had ever allowed herself to recall. Breathtakingly good-looking too, and very well aware of the fact. He was the type of guy she should have run a mile from. That she had not had the wit to run, that she had to her own everlasting shame ended up in his bed within hours of first meeting him, was a continuing source of deep mortification to her.

'I've come to make you an offer you can't refuse.'

'Oh, I can refuse, all right…there isn't anything you could offer me that I wouldn't refuse!' Tabby launched back at him as wildly as though he were offering her the seven deadly sins all packed together in one handy bag.

Unmoved, watchful, Christien studied her, his attention travelling from the tumbling mane of her caramel-blonde hair to her bright eyes and the freckles scattered across her slanted cheekbones. But his gaze lingered longest on the soft, vulnerable fullness of her mouth. He only had to look at her ripe pink lips to remember how the caress of them had once felt against his skin. As his body betrayed him by hardening in instantaneous response and he recalled that no other woman had since given him that much pleasure, but that she had gone behind his back with some lout on a Harley-Davidson, raw anger seized Christien without warning.

'You want to take a bet on that, *chérie*?' he demanded in his sexy, whiplash drawl.

CHAPTER TWO

'I DON'T bet on a certainty and I didn't ask you to come in!' Beneath the insolent onslaught of Christien's appraisal, Tabby's rounded face was burning like a furnace.

Nobody, but nobody, could do insolence as well as Christien Laroche did. Arrogant dark head high, he could elevate one satiric brow and make people feel about an inch tall. It was a talent that came from being the latest in the line of several hundred years of ancestors, every one of whom had thought of themselves as an exceptional being. Self-assured to a degree that was intimidating, Christien knew himself to be superior to most in intelligence and it could not be said that that knowledge had made him humble.

'But then you were never very good at saying no to me, *ma belle*,' Christien countered with silken sibilance.

Tabby flinched. Her hands snapped into small fists while he continued to look her over as though she were human flesh adorned with a sale board. His bold scrutiny lingered on the firm jut of her full breasts below the faded red T-shirt she wore and Tabby got even tenser. Beneath her bra, her own body was letting her down by reacting to his visual attention. As her tender nipples pinched into straining prominence, Tabby spun round and headed fast into the sitting room.

Already she could barely think straight. Christien had always had that effect on her but she was also feeling humiliated. How could she argue with him? She had never managed to say no to him, had never wanted to. She had been *enslaved*. Even though she had been a virgin when they had met, from somewhere inside her he had somehow brought out a secret slut whom she had never dreamt existed. He was the one male in the world whom she should never have met, for with him she had discovered she was without defence.

Christien would not allow himself to take further note of the effect of that faded red cotton stretching across her lethally bountiful chest. Expelling his breath on a slow, pent-up hiss of annoyance as he found himself wondering how she would react if he just reached for her as he had once done without thought, he planted himself several feet away from temptation. She was not beautiful, he reminded himself. Her nose was a little too large, her mouth a little too wide and she was way too short for elegance. But, for all that, put the whole lot together, throw in the freckles and the dimples that had once laced her glorious smile and he had wanted to veil her like an Arab woman and lock her up in a turret at Duvernay, to be seen, relished and enjoyed solely by himself. Remembering the fierce possessiveness she had once inspired him with, he was gripped by rare discomfiture.

'I would like to buy back the property which my great-aunt left you in her will,' Christien imparted coldly.

Even as he spoke Tabby lost colour. She studied the laminated wood floor, fighting valiantly to overcome a ridiculous sense of hurt and rejection. For what other reason would he have come to see her after so long? He could not even stand for her to own one miserable little piece of what had once been Laroche land and property. Well, that was his bad luck, Tabby thought with sudden anguished bitterness.

'I'm not interested in selling,' Tabby said tightly. 'Obviously, your great-aunt wanted me to have the cottage—'

'*Mais pourquoi*...but why?' Christien asked her. 'That still makes no sense to me.'

Tabby had no intention of telling him that she believed that his great-aunt had felt sorry for her because *he* had broken her heart! Or that, in her opinion, for the older woman to have felt so sympathetic she must once have suffered a similar experience of her own. 'I expect it was just a whim...she was a lovely person,' she framed tautly, for she very much wished that she had had another chance to meet the older woman.

'In France,' Christien drawled in his deep, dark voice, 'it is not the done thing to leave even a small portion of ground to someone outside the family. I am willing to pay well over the market price to ensure that the cottage remains a part of the estate.'

Raging, hurting resentment flared through Tabby, although she was trying very hard to stay calm. Unhappily, discovering the purpose of Christien's visit had only made that an even greater challenge. Three years ago, Christien had icily rejected her pathetic pleas for even a moment alone with him and she did not believe that she would ever forgive him for that. But now the same incredibly wealthy and privileged male was willing to approach her over the head of a cottage that his great-aunt had only used for summer picnics! His behaviour struck Tabby as being horribly cruel and unfeeling.

In any case, *she* might be an outsider but her son had rather more claim than she had to the property,

Tabby reminded herself doggedly. Jake's illegitimate birth might have placed him outside their precious family circle but, regardless of that reality, her son had Laroche blood in his veins and he was entitled to a home on French soil. In addition, Solange Roussel had not left Tabby that cottage on the expectation that she would sell it straight back to Christien sight unseen. To Tabby, the very idea of immediately disposing of her inheritance seemed ungrateful and horribly disrespectful to Solange's memory.

'I'm not selling.' Forcing her head up, Tabby connected with his scorching tawny gaze. That fast, a sensation of heat sprang up low in her pelvis and lit every sensitive inch of her flesh with a burning physical awareness of his masculinity that was a pure torment to bear.

'Take a look at the cheque first,' Christien invited, the words thick with his accent, slightly slurred, faint colour accentuating the hard angle of his bold cheekbones.

Blinking in surprise, mouth running dry, Tabby only then noted the cheque he had tossed down onto the dining table in front of the window. Her mind was a complete blank.

'Take the cheque and I'll take you out to lunch.' Christien was aching for her and wondering if he would even make it out of the house without giving way to the megawatt sexual vibes filling the atmosphere.

Where had she heard that before? In her time with him, how many lunches and dinners had she never received? They had not been able to resist each other long enough to reach the restaurant. Once they had ended up in a lay-by. Another time he had done a U-turn in the middle of the road, cursing and laughing at the strength of his desire for her. During their affair, she had lost a stone in weight and had felt lucky to get the chance to rifle the villa's fridge while he'd been asleep.

'I'll *try* to take you out to lunch...' Christien rephrased, golden eyes a smouldering gleam below sensually lowered lashes, his vibrant smile suddenly flashing out to chase the gravity from his sculpted mouth, for he was recalling that U-turn as well.

When he smiled that stunning smile, it brought back so much remembered pain for Tabby that it hurt her to look at him. Having won her release from his spellbinding gaze, she shivered, folded her arms tight in front of herself, suddenly cold and scared inside.

'No, thanks...please take your cheque and leave,' she told him unevenly.

'You don't mean that...you don't *want* that,' Christien purred with immense confidence, all caution thrown to the winds in the face of his own hunger.

No, but she knew that she would never forgive herself if she did not resist him. He had taught her that a level of wanting that went beyond the bounds of common sense or pride was destructive. That he was being his typical arrogant self also helped. He sauntered back into her life after years away and just assumed that she would be as eager for him as she had been at seventeen. But she *was*, wasn't she? And he could feel that in her too, she conceded with a sinking heart, for when had he not been able to read her like a book?

Filled with fear of her own weakness, Tabby said abruptly, 'Is Solange's cottage close to your home at Duvernay?'

Christien frowned. '*Non*...miles by road.'

'Do you go there often?'

In answer, Christien growled with impatience. 'No. I want you to sell. If it is your wish to own property in France, I will instruct an agent to find somewhere more suitable for you.'

'You have no right to demand that I sell!' Tabby snapped in sudden furious denial of all the frightening raw feelings that his very presence was making her relive. 'And who are you to decide what's suitable for me?'

'I can't imagine what you could want with a dwelling in the remoter depths of the Breton countryside. I doubt if it is even habitable. It *has* been almost half a century since the property was used as anything other than a glorified summer house!' In a raw gesture of impatience, Christien raked long, lean brown fingers through his luxuriant black hair. 'Why won't you see sense? Only a Laroche belongs on the Duvernay estate!'

Paling, Tabby turned her head away, wondering why she was letting him make her feel as if she were something less than he was.

'In any case,' Christien murmured in scornful addition, having read a message of poverty in her faded T-shirt and worn jeans, 'You look like the money would be a lot more use to you.'

'How do you know that? You know nothing about me now!' Tabby flung back fiercely, furious that he was putting her down like that. 'What I want...what I need, *anything*!'

Christien dealt her a brooding appraisal, anger at her unexpected stubbornness driving him, for once she had done exactly as he wished without hesitation. '*Au contraire*, I know many things about you that I would rather not know,' he contradicted with a harsh edge to his rich drawl. 'That you're a compulsive liar—'

'No, I'm not. I just told a few fibs. You never *asked* me what age I was!' Tabby argued, feverish colour mantling her cheeks as she surged to her own defence.

Christien aimed a look of raw contempt at her. 'That you can't even take responsibility for your own actions—'

'Shut up!' Tabby suddenly hurled at him, half an octave higher.

'And you still lose your head when you are confronted with your flaws—'

'And you think *you're* so perfect?' Tabby hissed at him, rage jumping up and down inside her.

'No, I wasn't perfect, *ma belle*,' Christien conceded in a black velvety purr, scorching golden eyes locked to her outraged face. 'But even when I was at my most rampant I never ran two lovers at one and the same time. Sleeping with the lout on the Harley-Davidson while I was in Paris was sordid and sluttish…and not a trifling offence I felt I could overlook!'

The silence was charged with hard, hostile vibrations.

Tabby was staring at his lean, strong face with wide eyes of appalled disbelief. 'Say that again…I mean, I *didn't*…I didn't do what you just said I did with *any* lout on a Harley!'

'*En voilà une bonne*…that's a good one! The compulsive liar bites again,' Christien derided with a curled lip.

Grim at that degrading recollection, he strode past her back into the hall.

In a daze at what he had just let drop, Tabby halted

in the sitting-room doorway. 'Did you really think I'd been unfaithful? How *could* you think that?'

'If you were easy with me, why shouldn't you be equally easy with someone else?' Christien lifted and dropped a shoulder, smouldering animosity laced with contemptuous dismissal in his insolent appraisal. 'And let us be honest…five days was a long time for you to go without sex, *chérie*.'

'I won't forgive you for talking to me like this—'

'I don't want forgiveness.' In fact, Christien felt forgiveness of even the most minor variety might be very, very dangerous to his own interests.

Tabby Burnside was nothing but trouble. She had no morals. That that should appeal to him was not a trait within himself that he ought to encourage. She would accept the cheque. Of course she would accept the cheque. However, if there were any further negotiations required, he would leave the matter in the hands of his English solicitor. After all, he was to marry to Veronique, who was a fine woman. Beautiful, honest, trustworthy. She would make an excellent wife. Eventually he would become a father and a grandchild might well lift his mother's spirits a little. Was that not what had prompted him to become engaged in the first place? Wild, hot sex, fights and seething attacks of emotion would never feature in his alliance with Veronique. That was *good*, Christien told himself.

For a long time after Christien had departed, Tabby stared into space. The lout on the Harley-Davidson? Could he have been referring to the English student, Pete? Pete and two of his mates had been staying nearby. Pippa and Hilary had become friendly with them and Tabby *had* gone out with Pete on his bike one evening when Christien had been in Paris. But that had been all. Why had Christien accused her of sleeping with Pete? How could he have believed that she would have behaved like that? Why would he have believed that when she had been so patently crazy about him?

Once more time was sliding back for Tabby and she was reliving that summer. After that first ennervating sighting of Christien in the village, Tabby had lived in a daydream inhabited only by her fantasy of Christien and herself. Her stepmother had become noticeably less unpleasant when Tabby had opted to stay behind at the farmhouse most evenings while everybody else had gone out. Tabby had gloried in the quiet and the privacy and the daring freedom of bathing naked in the big blue-tiled pool. She still remembered the wonderful cool of the water on her overheated bare skin. At the outset of the second week while she'd still been in the water swimming, the electricity had cut out.

Wrapped in a towel, she had been attempting to find her way through the rambling farmhouse back to her bedroom when she had heard a car pulling up outside. Assuming everyone had come back early, she had gone to the door, but it had been Christien out on the front veranda with a torch.

'I saw the lights go out and I guessed you'd be here alone. Join me for dinner, *chèrie*,' he murmured.

'But there's a blackout—'

'We have a generator.'

She stood there, teeth chattering with nerves, hair dripping round her. 'I'm all wet—'

'You would like me to dry you?'

'I'll need to get dressed.'

'Don't bother on my account.' In the light of the

torch, mocking tawny eyes set below the lush black fringe of his lashes rested on her hot face. 'Are you sure you're not too warm in that towel?'

'You don't even know my name. It's—'

'Not important right now.'

'Tabby,' she completed shakily, taken aback by the intensity of his appraisal.

'You don't look at all like a little brown cat. You're smaller than I thought you would be, too,' Christien confided, inspecting her with the torch beam. 'But you have fabulous skin. Don't bother with make-up. I hate it.'

For Tabby, his appearance was her every dream come true and she was terrified that he would disappear while she was getting dressed. Giving her the torch, he told her he would wait in the car.

'I don't know your name,' she said when she climbed into his car.

'*Naturellement*...of course you do,' he contradicted with disturbing confidence.

'All right...I asked one of the locals who you were,' Tabby mumbled.

'Don't waste your best lines on me. I've heard them all before and honesty is fresher.'

'I don't know you...I shouldn't have got into a car with you,' Tabby exclaimed, because she was suddenly feeling very much out of her depth in his company.

'But I feel I know you so well already, *ma belle*. Every night of the past four I have watched you strip off and cavort naked in the pool down here.'

At the news that her swimming sessions had not been as private as she had believed them to be, Tabby gasped in shock. 'I beg your pardon—?'

'Don't be coy. I respect nerve and enterprise in a

woman. I also admire a woman who knows what she wants and goes after it,' Christien breathed with a husky intimacy. 'And the simple ploy was remarkably effective…here I am.'

Her aghast embarrassment fought with her recognition of his apparent respect for what he had interpreted as an adventurous campaign to attract his attention. The temptation to pose as an enterprising go-getting woman triumphed over all common sense. She did not angrily demand to know how he could possibly have seen her bathing in a pool surrounded by a wall or ask him how on earth he could have sunk low enough to spy on her. She did not contradict his outrageously self-satisfied assumption that she had been breaking her neck to get off with him and, as mistakes went, hiding behind that fake image was her first mistake with Christien.

There was no great mystery about why she ended up in Christien's bed on their very first date either. She was so excited at dining alone with him in the incredibly opulent villa that she barely ate a mouthful but she *did* drink three glasses of wine. Nor did she have a prayer of resisting a guy with his seductive expertise. In fact she was a lost cause from the first kiss for nobody could kiss like Christien could.

'*Zut alors*…I am crazy for you,' Christien intoned with ragged emphasis, sweeping her off her feet in high romantic style as if she were not a healthy lump frequently scorned by her stepmother as being on the larger side of overweight. For that alone, for his simple ability to lift her without grunting with effort, she would have loved him.

'You enchant me,' Christien swore, so that she felt generous enough to try and hide the fact that the first time he made love to her and she lost her virginity without him noticing, it hurt. And when he seemed to suspect that things hadn't gone quite as well for her as he seemed to have expected, she pretended to go to sleep because she was so embarrassed.

So for her, it was not sex, it was *never* just sex, because the first night she went to sleep in his arms, she very much hoped that he would not want to do what they had just done very often. In the middle of the night, she crept out of the bed and he sat up and switched on the light. 'Where are you going?' he demanded.

'Er...back down the hill,' Tabby muttered, worried sick that Pippa would have reported her absence from the bedroom they shared.

'I don't want to let you go but...*Ciel!*' Christien groaned. 'What was I thinking of? To keep you this late was madness. How liberal are your family?'

Her father would have taken a shotgun to him without hesitation, but it would have been the opposite of cool to admit that. He was very disconcerted when she refused even to let him take her back in the car. She was even more dismayed when he insisted on walking her down the road to the very entrance of the farmhouse. 'Can I see you tomorrow morning for breakfast?' he asked.

'I'll try to make lunch—'

'You'll *try*? Was I that bad?' In the moonlight, Christien gave her a rueful grin that had so much charismatic appeal, it physically hurt her to leave him.

When she climbed in the window of the bedroom she was sharing with Pippa, Pippa was wide awake. 'Have you gone crazy?' the other girl hissed furiously. 'Did you think I wouldn't realise that you've been out all night with that guy in the flash sports car?'

'How did you find out?'

'I just watched you snogging him from an upstairs window! I'm been going out of my head worrying about you and wondering whether I ought to tell our parents you were missing,' Pippa censured angrily. 'What's got into you? Don't ever put me in a position like that again!'

What *had* got into her that summer? Tabby wondered with shamefaced regret. Mercifully, it had been a recklessness that had never touched her again. Disturbed by Tabby's unfamiliar behaviour with Christien, Pippa had moved into Jen's room instead. Tabby had been upset by her friend's defection, but not upset enough to turn her back on Christien. Her need for him had been all-consuming, her love total, and nothing and nobody else had mattered to her. Only living and breathing for him, she had slept through the daylight hours she'd often been away from him like a vampire in a coffin who only came into real being and secret life after nightfall.

Angry tears stung Tabby's eyes as she stared down at the cheque that Christien had left behind him. With hands that were all fingers and thumbs she tore it up into lots of little pieces. She had not even looked at it to see how much he had been prepared to pay for the cottage. He did not want her in France, but she had already made all her arrangements. How dared Christien assume that he could buy her off and make her do things she didn't want to do? How dared he call her easy to her face? *He* had betrayed *her*, but then he had never given her any promises of fidelity, had he? Nor, she noted, had he mentioned his staggeringly beautiful blonde Parisienne girlfriend.

She would go to Solange's cottage and she would

use it for as long as she wished. It would be a mark of
her respect for a sweet woman, whom sadly she had
never got to know well. Perhaps at the end of the summer she would take stock on whether or not anywhere
in the vicinity of Duvernay was the best place for her
to embark on a new life with her son. But as for
Christien Laroche, who had already caused her so
much grief, he had better steer clear of her from
now on!

CHAPTER THREE

A SLIM blond male of around thirty with steady blue eyes and an attractive grin, Sean Wendell walked Tabby back to the town car park. He groaned out loud when he realised what time it was. 'I'm going to have to rush off and leave you here…I have an appointment with a client.'

'No problem. You've been a terrific help and thanks for the coffee,' Tabby told him warmly, for her aunt's former work colleague had proved to be a positive goldmine of local knowledge.

Regardless of the fact that he was already running late, Sean followed her across to the ancient van packed high with possessions. He continued to hover while she climbed back into the driver's seat. 'Look, don't try to unload the van on your own,' he urged. 'I'll come over this evening and give you a hand.'

'Honestly, that's very kind of you but I loaded it up, so I should be able to unpack it again.' Colouring at the continued heat of Sean's admiring appraisal, Tabby closed the van door and drove off with a wave. She liked him but wished that he had taken the hint that, while she was always happy to have another friend, nothing more intimate was on offer.

It was four o'clock on a warm June afternoon. She had made good time from the ferry port and Sean's linguistic prowess had speeded up her dealings with the *notaire*. Now, she was barely twenty kilometres from her final destination. However, as Tabby drove out of

41

Quimper again a glimpse of a shop window full of colourful faience pottery sent her thoughts winging back to her childhood. Her late mother had collected the elegant hand-painted pottery for which the cathedral city was famed and every year a fresh piece had joined the display on the kitchen dresser. Shortly before their move to a new and much bigger house, Tabby's stepmother, Lisa, had disposed of the whole collection, along with everything else in the household that had reminded her of her husband's first wife. After her father's death, it had hurt Tabby to have no keepsakes with which to highlight her memories of her parents.

But on the day that she travelled through Brittany to claim her inheritance, it would have been impossible for her to forget that her mother's biggest dream had always been to own a house in France. Indeed, by the time that Tabby finally identified the half-timbered one-and-a-half-storey cottage that was screened from the quiet country road by a handsome grove of oak trees, she was very much in the mood to be excited and to be pleased with all that she saw.

The front door of her new home opened straight into a big room with a picturesque granite fireplace and exposed ceiling beams. It was full of character and Tabby smiled. Her smile dimmed only a little when she glanced through a doorway at a kitchen that consisted of a stone sink and an ancient range that did not look as though it had been lit in living memory. The washing facilities were equally basic. However, the final room on the ground floor came as a delightful surprise for it was an old-fashioned sun room with good light, which would make a wonderful studio for her to work in. Up the narrow twisting oak staircase two rooms lay under the eaves. She unlatched stiff windows to let in

the fresh air before strolling back downstairs and out
of doors.

The garden rejoiced in splendid countryside views,
an orchard and a pretty little stream. It would make a
wonderful adventure playground for Jake, Tabby reflected cheerfully. Having seen all that there was to see,
she endeavoured to take sensible stock of her inheritance. Christien's description of the property as a 'glorified summer house' had been infuriatingly accurate
for there was no central heating, no proper kitchen or
bath. She had also rather hoped that there would be
some furniture to supplement what little she had of her
own, but apart from a couple of wicker chairs in the
sun room the cottage was bare to the boards. On the
other hand, the roof and walls seemed sound, her utility
bills would be tiny and, once she was bringing in a
decent income, she would be able to add a few frills.

Her good mood very much in the ascendant, Tabby
sat down under a tree and took advantage of the pro-
visions she had bought on the outskirts of Quimper.
Her hunger satisfied by half a baguette spread with to-
matoes and ham and washed down with water, she
changed into shorts and a T-shirt in preparation for
cleaning the room where she planned to stay the night.
An hour later, every surface scrubbed, she unloaded her
bed from the van. As the head and footboards were
made of wood, getting them up to the bedroom was no
mean task, but she persevered and indeed was finally
struggling with what was left of her energy to drag up
the mattress as well when a knock sounded on the ajar
front door.

Having got the unwieldy double mattress squashed
round the bend in the staircase, Tabby was lying across
it to keep it there while she tried to catch her breath

again. Determined not to let go of the mattress, she attempted to twist her head round and peer down to see who was on the doorstep, but it was an impossible feat. 'Yes?' she called, praying that it would be Sean Wendell arriving as promised to offer his male muscle.

'It is I...' A dark-timbred masculine drawl imparted with accented clarity and awesome cool. 'Christien...'

She was unable to see him and taken badly by surprise; dismay provoked Tabby into loosing a rather rude word. It was ironic that it was a word that she had never said out loud in her life before and she cringed at her own lack of control over her wretched tongue. In fact she just wanted the ground to open up and swallow her and a fiery blush enveloped her complexion. Had he tried, Christien could not have chosen a worse moment to spring a visit on her.

Entering the cottage, Christien angled his proud dark head back and wondered if she had a man upstairs with her. 'Are you planning to come down and speak to me any time soon?'

Feeling trapped and foolish, Tabby flipped over and struggled to wedge the mattress in place while she stretched forward as far as she dared in an effort to see Christien. But that movement was all that it took for the bulky item to spring free of her hold. The weight of the mattress against her back dislodged her feet from the step and as the mattress forced its passage back down the stairs at shocking speed it carried her with it. In dismay, she cried out but it was too late: the edge of the heavy mattress hit Christien hard on the knees, destroyed his balance and toppled him before he could move from its path.

Christien fell and he only managed to partially break that fall by bracing strong hands on either side of her

startled face. Tabby was winded by the sheer impact
of a well-built six-foot-three-inch male hitting the mattress and momentarily crushing the life out of her lower
body.

'*Zut alors!*' Christien raked down at her with furious
force.

For an instant as she careened down the stairs like
a cartoon character on board a novel flying carpet the
world had swum scarily out of focus, but now it had
righted itself again and Tabby found herself gazing up
into dark golden eyes as bright as gemstones in a masculine face handsome enough to take any woman's
breath away. Her slight body stilled taut as a bow string
beneath the heavy imprint of his. Something as powerful as it was emotionally painful swelled inside her
chest and her throat tightened, her mouth running dry.
Physical memories were engulfing her to a level beyond bearing for her senses had gone off on a roller-
coaster ride of rediscovery.

The clean, evocative aroma that was unique to
Christien flared her nostrils: hard male heat braced with
a faint exotic hint of citrus. The very scent of his skin
was so immediately familiar to her that she was shaken
by the leap of her own recognition even at that most
primitive level. She searched his lean dark features, her
attention lingering on his level ebony brows, straight
nose, blunt cheekbones and stubborn jawline, and then
she connected with his amazing eyes again and felt a
deep, slow pulse begin a slow, dangerous beat way
down low in her pelvis. Below her T-shirt, her nipples
swelled and tightened into sudden embarrassing prominence. She didn't want to feel like that, indeed she
could barely credit that she could still react to the pri-
mal charge of his raw masculinity to such an extent,

but it was as though a chain reaction of response had kicked off inside her and, once started, there was no stopping it.

Tabby trembled, her hips succumbing to a tiny, involuntary upward shift and her slender thighs sliding a little further apart to better bear his weight in a movement as old as history itself. That wicked throb at the heart of her could not be denied even while she struggled to recapture her ability to think.

'What the hell do you think you are playing at?' Christien demanded wrathfully as in fierce, fervent denial of the burning heat of his own arousal, he began to lever himself up and back from her.

It was those words of his that were Tabby's ultimate undoing. The mere suggestion that she might somehow have choreographed a mattress to surf down the stairs and knock him off his feet was sufficient to send Tabby into a sudden helpless fit of giggles. Recalling how chillingly impressive Christien's air of grave authority had been before the mattress intervened, she was in stitches.

'You think this is funny...huh?' Christien growled with savage incredulity.

'I-Isn't it?' she prompted chokily.

A split second later, his hot, hungry mouth swooped down to possess hers and killed her near-hysterical amusement at source. He was pure erotic temptation. For the first time in almost four years, electrifying excitement seized Tabby. Her head spun and air rasped in her tortured throat. The explicit intrusion of his tongue in the moist interior of her mouth sent a wave of delirious hunger currenting through her slight body. Her last grip on reality snapped: suddenly she was reaching up to him and no longer a passive partner.

Her arms locked round his lean, hard frame, her hands rising to shape his broad shoulders before her fingers snaked higher and delved deep into the black silk luxuriance of his hair to hold him to her.

'Christien?'

'*Non…*' In an abrupt movement, Christien wrenched himself back from her again. Breathing raggedly, he stared down at her, his smouldering gaze blazing gold, febrile colour accentuating the savage line of his hard cheekbones, ferocious tension written into every hard, angular line of his lean, strong face. In one powerful movement he vaulted upright, but it took every atom of will-power he possessed to step back from her. That acknowledgement both outraged and shocked him but, more than anything else, he was disconcerted by an awareness of exactly *what* had ripped his formidable self-discipline to shreds a moment earlier: that husky laugh of hers had snatched him back in time to that summer.

He had never forgotten that streak of bubbling, contagious joy that was so much a part of her nature, her childish habit of giggling at the most inopportune moments and in the worst of places, or her mysterious ability to lift him from his darkest moods. Loner and cynic though he was, he had basked in that warmth of hers, the extravagant, trusting ease with which she seemed to love. His hard, sensual mouth set into a tough line. Love as she had offered wasn't worth a damn but the sex had been out of this world, he reminded himself with bitter amusement.

'Why did you touch me?' Tabby condemned shakily.

'Why do you think, *chérie*?' The thickened note in his sexy drawl sent a responsive shiver travelling down her taut spinal cord.

'You shouldn't have. That's all in the past.' Shaking like a leaf in a cruel wind, Tabby scrambled off the mattress and turned away from him. Her knees were wobbling and her hands were trembling. Her reddened lips stung from the devouring heat of his and more than anything else in the world she just wanted to sink back into the lean, powerful strength of him and taste him over and over again until the terrifying ache of loss he had filled her with had finally evaporated and faded like a bad memory.

And that was *not* how she should be thinking about a male who had once used her and discarded her again with no more care or consideration than he might have utilised had she given him her body in a casual one-night stand. In fact it was frightening to recognise the longing still pent-up inside her and the extent of her own vulnerability. Where were her pride and her intelligence?

'How did you even know I was moving in today?' she demanded, desperate to keep herself busy and stooping down to snatch at the mattress and manhandle it up onto its side again.

Someone who knew that she had an appointment to collect the keys from the *notaire* had made the mistake of passing on that news to Matilde Laroche and Christien's working day had been interrupted by his distraught parent and her announcement. He had left his mother in the soothing hands of her doctor but his own patience had been sorely tested. Only once in his life had his late father attended one of Solange's rustic picnic parties, so his son could not see how the overgrown meadow outside could be regarded by the older woman as being in quite the same category as sacred ground.

'I can understand that you would want to take a look at your inheritance,' Christien remarked with studied calm. 'Naturally you're curious but I can't believe that you're planning to live here.'

'Why can't you believe it?'

'*Pas possible*...it's not habitable!' he retorted drily.

Out of the corner of her eye, Tabby studied him. His silk business suit was a trendy black pinstripe of exquisite cut that accentuated his wide shoulders, narrow hips and long powerful thighs. He looked absolutely gorgeous and, without her even realising it, her sneaky covert glance had become a full-on stare. Cheeks reddening as he elevated a questioning brow at the intensity of her appraisal, Tabby hefted one corner of the bulky mattress up onto the bottom step of the stairs again and slung him an expectant look. 'Are you going to give me a hand with this?'

Complete disconcertion pleated his level brows.

'Of course, it must be hard to stay fit when you're in an office all day.' Tabby sighed.

An utterly unexpected slashing grin banished the gravity from Christien's lean dark face. 'Do you really think I'm about to fall for a bait that basic?'

Riveted to the spot by the sheer charisma of that knowing smile, Tabby tried and failed to swallow. Closing his lean, shapely hands into the mattress, he hauled it up the stairs, negotiated with ease the bend that had caused her such grief and came to a halt in the room where the bed frame already stood assembled. As she reached the doorway he settled the mattress down onto the frame.

'Where did you find the bed? On a dump?' he enquired.

'It's old but it's solid.' However, her bed had come

closer to the dump than she would ever have admitted. Virtually all of the elderly furniture and household effects in the van had come from her aunt's attic and garage, both of which Alison was clearing in preparation for letting her property.

'You still haven't told me what you're doing here,' Tabby reminded Christien as she bent to rifle the cardboard box of bedding in the corner and emerged with a folded sheet.

Christien studied the sheet she was unfurling and noted that it had been carefully mended with a slightly different colour of cloth. Did people still patch linen these days? He was more shocked than he would have liked to admit by the sight of that mended sheet. He had a vague Cinderella-like image of her sitting darning by candlelight and, in defiance of that unusually colourful flight of fancy on his own part, he spread his hands in a scornful gesture. 'Why are you wasting your energy with this? You *can't* live here—'

'*You* couldn't,' Tabby countered, tucking in the sheet at the corners with determined industry, because at least while she was attending to practicalities she was not gawping at him like a lovelorn schoolgirl. 'You'd be lost without your luxuries, but I'll quite happy getting back to basics—'

'That's a double bed...who are you planning to share it with?' Christien demanded without warning.

An image of Jake's warm little body sneaking in below the covers first thing in the morning to cuddle up to her crossed Tabby's mind and her green eyes softened and her lush mouth took on a tender curve as she thought of her son.

Raw anger flaring and tensing his hard dark features, Christien strode forward to scrutinise her with brilliant dark golden eyes. 'If you choose to live on the Duvernay estate, there will only be one man in your bed, and that man will be me...*tu comprends*?'

In rampant disbelief, Tabby straightened to stare at him. 'Are you out of your mind?'

'Is that what you wanted...is that why you're here?' Christien purred low and soft, though the sting of that insolent enquiry cut like glass against her tender skin. 'You want to take up where we left off that summer?'

Without even thinking about what she was going to do, powered by hot, deep anger alone, Tabby slapped him. The crack of her fingers against his bronzed cheek sounded preternaturally loud in the hot, still room. 'Does that answer that question?'

Christien was so taken aback by that physical attack that he fell back a step.

The shock in his stunning golden eyes was patent and Tabby flushed. 'You *made* me do that—'

Lean bronzed hands snapped over her wrists like handcuffs. 'Then I will have to make equally sure that you don't do it again.'

Tabby tried to pull free of his hold and failed. 'It *is* your fault that I hit you!' she condemned like a spitting wildcat in her frustration. 'You were very rude. I'm in my own house and I have every right to be here if I want to be. If you enter my home, I expect you to mind your manners—'

'Or you'll assault me?'

Still struggling without avail to slide her wrists free, she felt her face flame at that sardonic interruption. 'Can't I move to France without you getting the idea that I've only come here to chase you?'

Disturbingly, his wide, sensual mouth quirked. 'Perhaps I want to be caught, *chérie*.'

'But I don't want to get involved with you again—'

'*Non?*' Christien prompted in a husky undertone, employing his hands to draw her closer.

'*Non…*' Tabby told him insistently, but her heart was starting to beat very, very fast behind her ribcage.

'I can be very well mannered,' Christien murmured silkily.

'Not around me, you're not—'

'You burn me up, *mon ange…*' His arrogant dark head bent as he released one of her hands and raised the other to press his mouth to the centre of her small pink palm.

The heat of that teasing caress made her shiver. Time was running backwards for her. She pressed her thighs together on the hot, liquid sensation of melting at the very heart of her. Already she felt tender and swollen and shame pierced her as sharp as an arrow. She was passionate and so was he and once that had been a source of joy and discovery to her. She had believed that they were a perfect match, but now when she felt the blood run hot in her veins it scared her and she judged it a weakness in herself. As that almost unbearable longing for him held her there, her troubled gaze lingered on his downbent dark head. 'Don't do this…'

'Don't do what?' Christien husked. 'Don't do… *this*?'

He sank his other hand into her hair and tipped her head back to skim the very tip of his tongue over the full curve of her lower lip. His breath warmed her skin and she trembled.

'Or…*this*?'

He delved between her readily parted lips and she

jerked and moaned, only to be racked by a shudder of frustrated longing as he lifted his head again.

'Tell me what you want, *chérie*.'

Her hand reached up of its own seeming volition and sank into his black hair. Stretching up on tiptoe, she drew him down to her, for she wanted his mouth on hers so badly that it hurt to be denied it. With an earthy groan, he lifted her up to him and crushed her mouth under his before he strode forward and lowered her down onto the bed. The moment he pressed her down on the mattress, the frame gave and collapsed with the most enormous crash down onto the floor.

Christien swore and snatched her back up again from the tumbled mattress. Still holding her slight body taut to his broad chest in a protective stance, he stepped back to the doorway and surveyed the disassembled bed with incredulous force.

'I forgot...I still had to tighten up the screws holding the frame together,' Tabby mumbled unevenly.

'You could've been hurt.' Christien set her down on her own feet again.

'I'm glad it happened...it stopped us doing something stupid,' Tabby asserted tightly.

Firm male footsteps sounded on the staircase. 'Tabby?' a familiar voice called. 'Are you OK? I saw the door open and just came on in when I heard the noise.'

A relieved smile driving the taut tension from her generous mouth, Tabby flipped round Christien's stilled figure and went to the head of the stairs. 'Sean...you're very welcome and I'm about to take shameless advantage of you. Are you any good with a screwdriver?'

Dark eyes veiled, Christien surveyed the young

blond male with his self-satisfied smile and designer stubble and experienced a powerfully disturbing desire to kick him back down the stairs again.

'I brought my tool-kit with me...' Sean confided as he passed by Christien.

Christien was so pained that he almost winced. Who was this jerk?

'Sean...er, this is Christien.'

Neither man extended a hand. Each awarded the other a stiff but studiously casual nod.

Tabby tried not to notice that Christien made Sean look small, skinny and in need of a good shave.

'I'll sort the bed out...no problem,' the Englishman asserted, and started to whistle quietly.

'May I talk to you downstairs?' Christien murmured to Tabby.

Worrying at her lower lip, Tabby led the way, her slim back rigid.

'Is the whistling handyman going to be living here too?' Christien enquired flatly.

Tabby tensed. 'I don't think that's any of your business—'

'So I can just take care of him by going back up there and breaking his neck now, can I?' Christien incised.

Tabby paled in disbelief.

'I'm being straight. I don't want any other guy anywhere near you. Who is he?'

Tabby focused on scorching dark golden eyes and her mouth ran dry. 'You don't have the right—'

Christien swung back to the stairs. 'I'll go ask him—'

'*No!*' Tabby snapped in horror. 'He's a friend of my

aunt's and lives locally... For goodness' sake, I only met him today!'

As far as Christien was concerned at that moment, nothing that he himself had done or said since he entered the cottage seemed to have had the smallest intellectual input from his brain. But her admission that her visitor was only an acquaintance cooled the white-hot, irrational anger that he was fighting to restrain.

Tabby walked right out to the silver Ferrari parked at the side of the cottage. 'I want you to leave...and I don't want you to come back—'

'Don't lie to me—'

Her small hands closed into tight, hurting fists of self-control as she fought her own weak inclinations with all her might. 'I won't sell this place, I'm staying...that's *all* you need to know—'

'So that we can both lie awake on the hot nights?' By the simple dint of moving forward, Christien cornered her against the wing of the car and backed her into contact with the sun-warmed metal. 'Tell me now,' he instructed in a raw-edged undertone.

'No...' Almost mesmerised by the smouldering heat of his golden eyes, Tabby stared back at him, pupils dilated, body humming with wild, hot, wicked awareness.

'Say it like you mean it,' Christien urged in a ragged undertone, leaning forward even as she leant back.

The front door slammed with a loud thud that made both of them leap back from each other in sudden mutual discomfiture.

Sean Wendell angled an apologetic grimace at Tabby. 'Sorry...the wind caught it!'

'He's a smart ass,' Christien growled with barely restrained menace.

Her colour high, Tabby walked away without another word. She didn't dare look back at him, not when just turning her back on him had demanded almost superhuman will-power.

As the Ferrari drove off Sean rolled his eyes. 'Watching you two together is certainly an education—'

'Watching me with...Christien?' Tabby frowned. 'What are you talking about?'

'I don't think I've ever seen an attraction that powerful.' Sean remarked in wry fascination. 'I've just come out of a long-term relationship and now I know what was missing...the bonfire factor...stand back, feel the heat!'

Taken aback by the fact that her response to Christien was so painfully obvious that even a virtual stranger had recognised it, Tabby turned a fierce guilty pink. 'You misunderstood—'

'No, I don't think so, but I do know how to mind my own business.' With an easy grin, Sean asked her what she wanted to unload next from the van and she indicated the smart new furniture that she had bought specially for Jake's room in the hope of giving it greater appeal.

A couple of hours later, the van emptied, and alone again, Tabby stripped off and learned how best to wash her hair and all the rest of herself with only a sink and a saucepan to help with the task. As she climbed into her old-fashioned bed her thoughts were still full of Christien. The lure of the past always hit her hardest in weak moments: she was forever looking back to try and pinpoint the exact moment when her fairytale fantasy of everlasting happiness had begun to crack...

At the end of her third week of holiday, and a week

of being with Christien, his friend Veronique had called in for a visit. Christien had been talking on the phone and Tabby had been lying half asleep with her head on his lap. She still recalled glancing up to see the lovely brunette in her trendy beige linen dress standing in the doorway with her bright smile and her even friendlier wave. Veronique had seemed so very *nice*, Tabby recalled with a rueful grimace. And of course, being just seventeen, Tabby had taken Veronique at face value and the other woman had found it easy to win her trust.

'I thought I'd find Eloise in residence...I shouldn't be saying it,' Veronique whispered like Tabby's new best friend the minute Christien went out of hearing, 'but I've been dying for Christien to meet someone new and you look so *happy* together! Oh, please don't get me into trouble by saying I mentioned her!'

It had taken Christien's childhood playmate only half an hour to plant the first seeds of distrust and insecurity. In no time at all, Tabby was hearing about the gorgeous Parisienne model whom Veronique had assumed Christien was still seeing, and the clever brunette was offering useful little nuggets of supposed girlie wisdom concerning Tabby's relationship with him...

'I don't want to butt in *but* I think I ought to warn you that Christien really hates being pawed all the time.'

'Mention other boyfriends...he loves competition.'

'He has a very short attention span where women are concerned...'

Of course, with a few well-placed questions it was not difficult for Veronique to penetrate Tabby's masquerade of being a twenty-one-year-old student at art college. Christien had never asked for any details.

Why, oh, why had she ever pretended to be something she wasn't? Tabby asked herself unhappily. Why had she not sat down and thought before she'd parted her silly lips and lied about who and what she was to Christien the very first time that they'd spoken? She had believed that no guy in possession of a Ferrari and a fantastic villa would be interested in dating a seventeen year old fresh out of school. In her lively imagination, she had fast-forwarded her real life into the life she expected to be living four years in the future. After that initial bout of creative fiction, little more pretence had been required from her for they enjoyed a relationship rooted very much in the here and the now.

Until the final week when Christien went off to Paris on business, they had not spent a single day apart. There had been nobody to question where she was or what she was doing, for her father had been challenged enough to cope with his youthful bride's temper. In fact the older man had always seemed to be either hungover or on the way to getting hung-over again, Tabby recalled with painful regret. Thanks to Lisa's tantrums their family friends had engaged in a frantic round of activity in an effort to gloss over the reality that they were on the holiday from hell. Only the other teenagers in the party had understood that something more than a shrewish stepmother and a desire for her own space had been powering Tabby's preference for remaining at the farmhouse alone every day and every evening.

'What do you like most about me?' Tabby asked Christien dreamily one evening.

'How do you know I like anything?' Christien laughed out loud when she mock punched his ribs before saying with striking seriousness, 'You never try to be something you're not. What you see is what you get with you and I really appreciate that…'

She was all smiles until it finally dawned on her that what he had just admitted ought to strike cold fear into her veins, because a male who prized honesty and sincerity was unlikely to be impressed by a teenager who had told him a pack of lies in an effort to seem more mature and sophisticated than she was. During those final days she was feeling very insecure because Christien *had* become quieter and more distant with her, making her suspect that he was getting bored with their relationship.

'I think he's going off me,' she confided brittily to Solange on that second visit to the older woman's villa further up the valley.

'Christien has a very deep and serious nature,' his great-aunt soothed. 'Complex men are not easy to understand, especially when they're young and hot-headed.'

When just a few days later the embarrassing truth of Tabby's true age was 'accidentally' exposed by Veronique, Christien hit the roof and unleashed a temper that Tabby had never realised he had. Perhaps, however, her worst moment of humiliation occurred when, without any forewarning whatsoever, Christien came down to the farmhouse determined to finally meet her relatives. Lisa wandered in topless from the pool to flirt with him and a drunken argument then broke out between her father and her stepmother. Christien was excessively polite and reserved. Agonisingly aware of the distaste he was concealing, Tabby shrank with shame on her family's behalf.

'Do I still consider myself dumped?' she asked in

desperation as Christien climbed back into his elegant car.

'I went into this too fast. I need to think,' he ground out, capturing her willing mouth for a breathless instant that blew her away and then peeling her off him again with a grim look of restraint etched on his lean, strong face. '*Without* you around.'

'Don't expect me to sit around waiting for you!' she warned him shakily, suddenly very, very scared at the new distance she sensed in him and the tough self-discipline he was now exerting in her vicinity.

Christien sent her a truly pained appraisal that made her squirm. 'You sound so juvenile. I can't believe it took someone else to point out what I should have seen for myself.'

He went to Paris and he neither phoned nor texted her. Veronique implied that he was heading for a reunion with Eloise, who had spent most of the summer working in London. Tortured by his silence, Tabby was thrown back into the company of her friends for the first time that holiday. She did her utmost not to parade the reality that her heart was breaking. She never dreamt that the next time that she would see Christien, it would be in a hospital waiting room in the immediate aftermath of an unthinkable tragedy that left no space whatsoever for personal feelings or dialogue…

A towel knotted round his lean hips and still damp from the shower, Christien gazed unseeingly out the tall bedroom windows that gave the vast frontage of the Château Duvernay such classical elegance.

The mere awareness that Tabby was only a few fields away on the edge of the rolling parkland that surrounded his ancestral home was making him restless. Thinking about her unshaven caller, Sean, it was finally dawning on Christien that he had just walked out and left Tabby alone with a strange man. A strange man with the hots for her as well. Wasn't there something weird about a guy who went visiting with a tool-kit clutched in one hand? And might not some men misinterpret Tabby's naturally playful friendliness as a come-on? *Mon Dieu*, why hadn't it immediately occurred to him that Tabby might be at risk? He had left her at the mercy of a smirking handyman who might be a real sicko! Discarding the towel, Christien began pulling on clothes.

Dim light could be seen burning both upstairs and downstairs in the cottage. Swinging out of his car, Christien walked up the path and then paused beside a gnarled tree to check out the hole in the trunk. He drew out a dusty key and then with a frown returned it to its hiding place again. Strong jawline at a determined angle, he made loud and clear use of the door knocker…

CHAPTER FOUR

WHEN the knocker sounded, Tabby was curled up dozing on the wicker chair that she had brought through from the sun room.

Startled into wakefulness, she almost leapt out of her skin. Who the heck would come calling after midnight? Ought she to answer the door so late? Snatching up the bright patchwork crochet blanket she had draped over the chair, she wrapped it round herself, for she was only wearing a camisole nightdress.

It was Christien, black hair tousled by the faint breeze, brilliant golden eyes locking to her. Thud, bang, *crash* went her heartbeat, while her tummy seesawed as though the floor had dropped away below her. Eyes glinting a glorious green from below a feathery fringe of tumbling hair the colour of honey, she stared out at him, soft, full mouth damp and pink.

'Why have you come back?' Tabby whispered unevenly.

Christien did not even need to think about that. He had come back because he could not stay away. He closed the door behind him. He reached out and detached her fingers from the colourful blanket. Thick black lashes cloaking his gaze, he slid the blanket slowly down from her narrow shoulders.

'Christien...?' she queried unsteadily.

His breath rasped in his throat as he scrutinised her lush, inviting curves. Unquenchable lust gripped him in a hold tougher than any vice. White cotton moulded

her high, full breasts and the fabric was too thin to hide
the rosy prominence of her nipples. He wanted to touch
her, taste her, drive her insane with the same desire
that burned in him. 'If Sean had still been here with
you...I think I'd have ripped the bastard limb from
limb,' he confided not quite levelly.

Tabby whipped the blanket back up round her again
but her hands were shaking. 'I don't sleep around...I
never have and I never will. You had no reason to think
he'd still be here, but even if he had been it would be
none of your business—'

'But I'd have made it my business, *ma belle*.'

Although she knew she should not, she looked up at
him. The smouldering intensity of his dark golden gaze
set off every sensual alarm bell she possessed but she
moved not an inch. Indeed, she felt incapable of moving. For almost four years she had concentrated all her
energies on being a loving mother to Jake and studying
for her degree at art college. She had had to push herself very, very hard to cope as a single parent and a
student, who also needed to work a part-time job. There
had been little space for dating in her gruelling sched-
ule, but then that had not really been a sacrifice when
no ordinary male could dislodge Christien from her
mind. Christien with his black hair falling over his
bronzed brow, danger flashing gold in his stunning
eyes, not a single note jarring the sheer, riveting perfection of his hard, all-male beauty. Christien, the ultimate of impossible acts to follow.

Dry-mouthed, she settled her focus back on the real
live male in front of her. 'Why do you want to make
me your business again?'

'I don't know.' A rough, humourless laugh was

dredged from Christien. 'It's madness…but I'm still here.'

It shook her that Christien should say it was madness to be with her again and yet stay. He was mere inches from her, drop-dead gorgeous and virile and, that close to him, she felt boneless.

'You should leave—'

'Should but *won't.*'

'Is that a threat or a promise?' she whispered.

'What do you want it to be, *mon ange*?'

His presence was both threat and promise and she knew it. She had never stopped wanting him, had never learned to hate him. How could she when she understood the very forces that had ensured they stayed apart? The enormity of the tragedy that had engulfed their families that summer had shattered the tenuous remains of their relationship.

'What do I want?' She wanted him, only him. It was a truth that was rooted so deep in her that even pride could not make her deny it. 'Take a guess…'

Eyes shimmering hard and bright, Christien snatched in a ragged breath. He reached out and lifted her right off her feet and up into his arms in a demonstration of confidence and unapologetic masculine strength that made her feel weak and wanton and dizzy.

He took her mouth with stormy hunger and pried her lips apart to ravish the tender interior. A violent shiver of response racked her. Her heart hammering, she stretched up to him to deepen that connection. It felt so good she was instantly, helplessly addicted to her own craving for more. He pinned her up against the wall and his tongue plunged and withdrew between her readily parted lips with fierce, driving hunger.

Wrenching her stinging lips from his with a mighty

effort, she shut her eyes, fighting to maintain even a shred of restraint. 'The whole world's spinning,' she mumbled.

In an almost clumsy movement that bore little resemblance to his usual sure, fluid grace, he peeled her back off the wall and clamped her to his big, powerful length. He held her tight, so tight she could barely squeeze air into her constricted lungs.

'I'm sorry...I feel out of control,' he grated.

Her arms linked round him then and a smile like the sunrise started inside her where he couldn't see it. This was the guy who rarely took more than one glass of alcohol because feeling anything other than in total command of himself was anathema to him. To make him feel out of control even momentarily was an achievement of no mean order and to hear him confess it was a joy.

'I'm never in control with you,' she whispered back with neither resentment nor pleasure, just acceptance that that should be the case.

Christien felt light-headed with a triumph as old as time itself. She was his, she was still *his*. He was not a guy who reasoned in what he believed were primitive sexist terms and he had never felt possessive around any other woman. But she was different and, with her, he was different too and that was a conundrum he had never wasted any time agonising over. He set her down in the bedroom where an old Anglepoise lamp burned on an upturned box next to the bed. He did not think of himself as imaginative but he was already picturing the bare room furnished with the kind of pretty feminine clutter she adored.

Eyelids sensually lowered over his dark golden gaze, Christien treated her to a fierce, intent appraisal that fired her very skincells with awareness of her womanhood. 'I take one look at you and I'm so hungry for you I'm in agony,' he confessed huskily, sinking down on the edge of the bed and drawing her forward to stand between his spread thighs.

Was that why he was still so very special to her? Tabby asked herself. His ability to look at her with a wondering appreciation that suggested that she was an incredibly gorgeous woman when she herself knew that she was just an ordinary one? A marvel made all the more striking by the simple fact that Christien himself was very much in a class of his own? Even in well-worn jeans and a beige cotton sweater, he exuded exclusive cool and bred-in-the-bone sophistication. He possessed that degree of pure masculine good looks more often seen on a movie screen. Men of his ilk usually gravitated towards classically beautiful women, but she was wildly, humbly grateful that something she couldn't see and couldn't begin to understand had brought him to her instead.

Vulnerable and almost dazed by the intensity of her own emotions at that instant, Tabby looked back at him. 'Christien…?'

'You're very lovely, *ma belle*,' he said thickly, reaching up to tug the band out of her naturally curly caramel-coloured hair.

'I'm not—'

'Shush…' He finger-combed her hair down onto her taut shoulders, leant forward to let his tongue penetrate between lips as sweet and inviting as juicy strawberries.

She shivered and leant into that kiss, knees wobbling under her, hands suddenly coming down to steady herself on his long, powerful thighs. The swollen tightness of her nipples hurt. The very thought of his expert hands on her made her tremble with eagerness and already she was way beyond rational thought or restraint.

'Please…' she heard herself say.

'I want to take my time…I've pictured this too often,' he murmured roughly.

Mesmerised, she stood there, gazing into gorgeous golden eyes shaded by luxuriant black lashes longer and more luxuriant than her own. Just like Jake's, she conceded, and her throat tightened and she knew that she would have no choice but to tell him about his son now. Intimidated by the thought, she blanked out her mind.

Reaching up, Christien brushed the camisole straps down over her slim forearms, baring the proud, creamy swell of her breasts. The fabric caught on the taut rosy peaks. On fire with wanting, she felt her nightdress fall to her hips and he vented an earthy groan of bold appreciation.

'Stop looking at me like that…' she gasped, racked by shamed embarrassment for the terrible hunger that kept her standing there, exposed and desperate for his touch.

'I can't…you *are* exquisite,' Christien ground out, hauling her to him and closing his mouth to a pouting pink nipple.

All the breath pent-up inside her escaped in a startled gush, her soft lips parting, her head falling back, sweet, intense sensation thrumming through her in a heady tide while the moist heat at the heart of her quickened. His hands on her rounded hips, he roved from one stiff, sensitive bud to the other and she whimpered in response to urge him on. There was only him and what he could make her feel, and what he could make her feel drove out all else.

Long fingers shaping and moulding her tender breasts, he took her lush mouth again and again and the hard, male urgency of his plundering kiss wiped her out. She clung, gasped, felt the nightdress fall away and cried out low in her throat as he let sure fingers explore the slick, wet flesh between her thighs. She was trembling, utterly seduced by the screaming demands of her own body. He brought her down on the bed and stood over her while he hauled off his sweater with something less than cool.

'*Ciel*...I forgot how it feels with you, *ma belle.*' Dark colour accentuating his proud cheekbones, he studied her with raw intensity.

'I've never forgotten.' Tabby was deliciously, wickedly aware of the size and the strength of his big, powerful body and the hard ridge of male arousal jutting below the tight jeans he wore left her weak with wanting. Belatedly conscious of her own nudity and the golden eyes flaming hungrily over her, she curled her legs up and he gave her a slashing smile of wicked amusement.

She could not take her eyes off him. His lean bronzed torso bore a triangular pelt of black curls across his pectorals. He was powerfully muscled but as sleek in movement as an athlete. His stomach was washboard-flat and dissected by a silky furrow of dark hair. She watched him unsnap his jeans, skim them down to reveal boxers and long, hair-roughened thighs and the shame of her own excitement almost overwhelmed her.

'You make me crazy for you...' Christien groaned,

his rasping, sexy accent sending an evocative quiver down her spine.

He pulled her back to him. He made a praiseworthy effort to be cool, seductive and slow the pace with some seductive kissing, but her tongue twinned with his and he shuddered against her and ground his aching shaft into her pelvis with a raw growl low in his throat. Suddenly she was flat on the bed and he was devouring her with a wild, ravaging kiss. Her hunger went rocketing up the temperature scale and she rose up under him and sobbed his name below his marauding mouth, back arching in an agony of longing as he worshipped her breasts with his lips and his teeth.

'Please—'

'If I don't wait, I'll blow it,' Christien grated in raw warning.

'No...you won't.' She would have told him anything.

'*Oui*...just like the first time, like a stupid, over-eager kid, I'll *hurt* you!' Fabulous bone structure rigid, Christien glowered down at her as he struggled to maintain a grip on his fast-shredding control.

'That wasn't your fault.' Tabby pressed her lips to his strong jawline in a soothing gesture as natural to her with Christien as living. 'It was my first time and I should've told you but I was too embarrassed.'

Christien blinked. Her *first* time? When they met she had been a...virgin? One hundred per cent innocent, pure and untouched? And he hadn't noticed? He was stunned by the belated awareness that somewhere deep down where he had had no desire to probe he had always had that suspicion, but had never taken it out and faced it before. Why not? Was it possible that he had been reluctant to accept that amount of responsibility?

'Christien…?'

Golden eyes haunted by rare guilt, he steeled himself to back off, but her small hands were sliding into his hair, shaping his skull, and he looked down into luminous green eyes and fell victim to their enchantment instead. The drugging collision of their mouths ignited the hunger to a frantic fever again and her desperation only increased when he probed the hot, satin sensitivity between her thighs. She was in sensual torment, arching up to him, begging for more with every fibre of her being.

'I need to be inside you…' Dark blood delineating his hard cheekbones, Christien dragged her under him.

He plunged his swollen member into her damp, heated core and thrust deep. Sensual shock momentarily held her still. She could feel him stretching her and it had been so long that her own excitement was almost unbearable. His pagan possession thrilled her to the depths of her wanton soul. Her blood roared through her veins and her heart thundered as he drove her into his stormy rhythm. She was flying higher than she had ever flown and then she was crying out his name and her body was jerking, convulsing, breaking apart in a sweet, sweet rush of ecstasy. It felt so good, so wonderful it almost hurt and a surge of tears stung her eyes. His magnificent body shuddered over hers and she clutched him tight in the aftermath. It was as if she had been in suspended animation for almost four years and had suffered a sudden revival. She was in shock.

Christien emerged from the wildest, hottest orgasm of his life and struggled just to breathe again. He rolled over, carrying her with him, and stared down at her in a daze, pushing her tumbled honey-coloured hair back off her flushed, oval face with a lean brown hand that he noticed was trembling. That shook him even more.

Tabby drank in the musky, sexy scent of his damp skin and revelled in the familiarity even as a little voice shrieked inside her that she had just committed an act of insanity.

Christien pressed his lips to her smooth brow and rearranged her slight body over him. 'Once is never enough with you—'

'Don't be greedy,' she teased, snuggling into him like a homing pigeon, determined not to think about what she was doing.

'I should have guessed that you were a virgin when we met,' Christien breathed, for he was only just beginning to disentangle that startling reality from the miasma of misinformation with which he had deliberately fenced his memories of her in the intervening years.

'You didn't want to know...you thought it might commit you in some way,' Tabby whispered abstractedly. 'I told myself you hadn't noticed but I was really just trying to explain what I wasn't old enough to understand.'

It had been almost four years since Christien had been treated to that amount of blunt honesty and his even white teeth momentarily gritted together. As a rule women wrapped up the unpalatable truth around him and never ever voiced it. 'It wasn't like that...'

Of course, it had been, Tabby reflected painfully. She had been besotted, out of her depth and trying to be something she was not and he had taken what all young, virile males were programmed to take: sexual conquest of a willing woman. Everything that had happened between them had been inevitable according to their sex, right down to her having fallen head over heels in love and him having got bored with her.

'It was…and you got bored—'

His long, lean length had turned very tense. 'I didn't get bored…you went off with the lout on the Harley.'

'I *didn't*—'

Christien lifted her off him and dumped her down onto the mattress by his side. 'For once in your life, tell the truth—'

Infuriated, Tabby sat up. 'I *am* telling the truth!'

'Where is the bathroom?' Christien demanded.

'Downstairs.' Tabby compressed her lips, green eyes fiery. 'I went out for a ride with Pete, and Pippa and Hilary were with his friends on their bikes. It was just a night out and nothing happened—'

'*Ciel!* Don't give me that! I saw you snogging him in the village…little slut!' Christien suddenly shot at her with a passionate fury that took even him aback and was a far cry from the cool he preferred to show the world.

Tabby froze while Christien sprang out of bed and hauled on his jeans. She remembered that as she'd clambered off the motorbike that evening Pete had leant forward and kissed her before they'd parted. It had lasted only a second and she had not wanted to shoot him down in flames in front of his mates and hers by making a three-act tragedy out of something so small.

'You saw that…' she gasped in genuine horror. 'Oh, *no*!'

Unimpressed, Christien sent her a sizzling look of derision. 'Did you do it on the bike with him the same way you laid yourself across the bonnet of my car for me?'

'Don't be disgusting!' Tabby launched at him in a rage of quivering mortification and then she fell still again, agile brain working fast. It was like a missing piece of jigsaw puzzle suddenly slotting into place for her. But unlike with the average jigsaw that missing piece had changed the whole picture. Taken in isolation, what Christien had seen must have looked damning. During that week, he had been away in Paris and he hadn't been in touch and then he had seen her kissing someone else.

'Why on earth didn't you confront me?' Tabby slung at the lean bronzed back heading down the stairs.

'You think I would lower myself to that level?' Christien shot back at her in disbelief.

Tabby almost screeched her frustration out loud and raced in his wake.

Christien emerged in shock from his brush with the primitive plumbing facilities. 'There is no place to wash!' he condemned with incredulity.

'There's a sink and a geyser that gives hot water…I want to talk about Pete—'

'So that was his name…' Christien snarled. 'You tart!'

'Stop it!' Tabby launched at him. 'My friends were there and so were his and it was broad daylight. I went for a spin on his bike…that's all. That stupid little kiss you saw was all that *ever* happened between us!'

'You think I am about to believe *that*?'

'Why not? I didn't kiss him back but it didn't even last long enough for me to push him away…it was innocent. I was nuts about you—'

'And the biggest liar in Europe!' Christien countered with crushing effect.

She paled and then flushed beet-red with guilt for it was unanswerable. 'But not about that,' she persisted tautly. 'I wouldn't have gone with any other bloke and you should have known that. But then maybe you did and you just needed another excuse to put me out of your life.'

Christien swore in French but he had stilled too and doubt was touching him for the first time. Back then he too had believed she was too keen on him to stray. However, at the time newly aware of just how young she actually was, he had also known just how short-lived a teenage infatuation could be.

'Then you got the ultimate excuse to stay away, didn't you?' In Tabby's anguished gaze was the terrible memory of their meeting like strangers in the hospital waiting room thronged with those whose lives had been damaged by Gerry Burnside's drunk driving and for ever shadowed by the lost lives of those who had not survived that night.

Gerry Burnside had driven round a corner on the wrong side of the road and he had crashed the four-wheel drive head-on into Henri Laroche's Porsche. Tabby's stepmother, Lisa, had been the only adult who had not been in her husband's car and she had been having hysterics in the waiting room. Pippa had been shattered by the death of her mother and waiting to hear how the emergency surgery on her father had gone. Hilary and her little sister, Emma, had been huddled together, bereft of both their parents. Jen's mother had been badly injured as well and Jen had been praying for her survival.

Christien had appeared with Veronique Giraud, his

beautiful dark eyes bleak with shock and grief, and Tabby had wanted to go to him to hold him, but she had not had the nerve to reach out in that moment to the man she loved, who had lost his father through her father's drunken, inexcusable recklessness at the wheel.

'My father's death…the crash…it would never have kept me from you.' Lean strong face taut, Christien hauled her into the sheltering circle of his strong arms.

'I wasn't involved with Pete,' Tabby told him again, determined to make him listen to her.

Christien knotted one hungry hand into her hair and kissed her breathless, shutting out the uneasy feelings she had stirred up. He had no desire to rehash the past. All he could think about was the next time he would be with her and the time after that and how often he would be able to fly up from Paris to be with her. Here in his great-aunt's summer house on the Duvernay estate? Impossible! He would find her a much more suitable and far superior property elsewhere…

Somewhere in the early hours, Tabby opened her eyes and moaned with helpless pleasure beneath Christien's expert ministrations. 'Again…?' she mumbled, marvelling at his stamina and luxuriating in him being so demanding too.

'Are you too tired?' His gorgeous accent was as effective on her as the effortless way he had managed to turn her liquid with longing even while she was still half asleep.

'Don't you dare stop,' she muttered and he laughed huskily and pushed her to fever pitch before he finally, mercifully answered the great shameless tide of hunger he had roused and left her limp and dazed with an overload of satisfaction.

When Tabby wakened again, dawn had been and

gone and when she stretched she discovered a dozen aches in secret places. She flipped over to survey Christien while he slept. Black lashes curled against a bronzed cheekbone, blue black stubble roughened his handsome jawline. The sheet was twisted round his hip, a muscular, long brown arm and a slice of hair-roughened chest exposed. Her chin resting on her folded arms, she suppressed a dreamy sigh. It was as if time had gone into reverse and she didn't really want to wake up and acknowledge the older, wiser individual she was supposed to be four years on.

He was the father of her son, so it wasn't surprising that she had never been able to forget him. In any case, it now seemed clear that only a stupid misunderstanding had separated them that summer. Such a little thing too that she could almost have screamed her frustration to the heavens: he had seen Pete kiss her and had assumed she'd been cheating on him. Of course that was Christien: the supreme pessimist and cynic always expecting the worst. Her lush mouth quirked. Oh, yes, she now understood why he would not even spare her five minutes on the day of the accident enquiry. His fierce pride would never allow him to overlook or forgive betrayal. For the first time, she also saw that the very ferocity of his rejection then had been revealing.

Last night, she had slept with him again. Over and over and over again. She was shameless, but she knew that if he woke up she still wouldn't say no to him. He was the only guy she had ever slept with but she was literally his for the asking every time and if she still loved him—and she suspected she did—was that so bad? Especially when fate seemed to be giving them a second chance? Or was it Solange who had given them a second chance? Had the older woman guessed that when she left the cottage to Tabby it would bring Christien into contact with her again?

Tabby smiled because a crazy happy feeling was bubbling up inside her. But then she tensed again for there was no denying that Christien was in for a major shock when she told him about Jake. She decided that she would prefer to spend some time with Christien *before* she made her big, stressful announcement. Just for one day, she bargained with her conscience, so that they could rediscover their relationship and sort out any other misunderstandings before she delivered the news that he was also the father of her three-year-old son. How was he likely to feel about that? Appalled? Pleased? But wasn't she rather putting the cart before the horse as well as being very presumptuous? What if…Christien had made love to her again out of simple lust? What if he just wanted to walk away from her again when he woke up? What if what they had just shared meant nothing at all to him?

Pale as parchment and feeling sick at that potential scenario, Tabby averted her gaze from him and crept out of bed. When she checked her watch, she grimaced for it was already almost nine. She had loads and loads of things to get done and very little time in which to accomplish them. Tomorrow she had to leave early to catch the ferry back to England again, she reminded herself doggedly. Lifting her overnight bag, she headed downstairs to freshen up and get dressed. She would call Alison from the public phone box she had noticed in the village and speak to Jake. She had to buy in wood and get the range going as well as stock up on basic groceries. In little more than a week's time she would be bringing Jake back over to France with her and she needed to make the cottage as welcoming as possible for his benefit.

Ought she to leave a note for Christien explaining where she had gone and when she hoped to be back from her errands? Wouldn't that make her seem a little clingy and desperate? She winced, feeling too vulnerable to lay herself open to the risk of rejection. It was better to do nothing at all. He knew where she was and he would have to go home for breakfast anyway as there was no food whatsoever in the kitchen. In any case, when she had made love with him the night before, she conceded painfully, she had demonstrated a remarkable ability to overlook the biggest stumbling block between them: the horrid accident in which his father had died. No matter how Christien felt, she was certain that his family would react to the news of his renewed involvement with her, not to mention the reality of her son's parentage, with horrified disgust. Fifteen minutes later, Tabby drove off.

She was recalling how, at the accident enquiry, Solange had made an embarrassed attempt to excuse her relatives' palpable hostility towards Tabby. 'My niece, Christien's mother, is under sedation today. Her suffering is terrible,' the old lady had confided. 'We all grieve for Henri, but in time the family will appreciate that many other people have also lost loved ones.'

When Christien wakened, he was surprised to find himself still at the cottage and even more surprised to find himself alone. He never, ever stayed the night with a woman. He could not initially credit that Tabby could have gone out and left him and he entered the sun lounge from which he had a clear view of the garden before he accepted that she was nowhere to be found. The bright room was cluttered with all the paraphernalia of an artist and when he saw the miniature painting on display he stopped to study it in some amazement. He had never seen anything so tiny, perfect and detailed as that landscape. At least, not outside the giant elaborate doll's house that his mother had made her lifetime hobby. If the miniature canvas was of Tabby's creation, she was very talented, but he was convinced that she had to be wrecking her eyesight painting in such a minute scale and he knew he would waste no time in suggesting that she concentrate her skills on larger creations.

She must have gone out to buy something for his breakfast, Christien decided. He wandered back up to the bedroom and strode to the window when he heard a car. A silver Mercedes coupé had drawn up on the other side of the road. A slight frownline divided his level dark brows for Matilde Laroche owned a car very similar, although she had not driven herself anywhere since his father's death. At the same time, he could not help but uneasily recall her hysterical overreaction the day before to the revelation that Tabby was taking possession of Solange's property. His Ferrari was sitting parked out front. Really, really discreet, Christien, he mocked himself. *Bon Dieu*, it was madness to even let it cross his mind that his ladylike parent might be so off the wall that she would lurk outside the cottage like some weird kind of stalker! Even so, suddenly he was very keen to see the car registration, but by the time he reached the front door the Mercedes had driven off again.

Initially, Christien made the most of his time alone to make several calls on his mobile phone and arrange a trip to a property in the Loire Valley. It was picturesque and secluded and enjoyed spectacular views.

Tabby was sure to leap at his offer because it would be certifiable insanity to do anything else. When another thirty minutes passed without her reappearance, he started to worry that something might have happened to her. Suppose she had climbed into that clapped-out old van and forgotten that his countrymen drove on a different side of the road from the British? He paled. Jumping into his car, he headed for the village a couple of kilometres away. Tabby would have passed through it the day before and if she had gone out to buy food, it was the most obvious destination.

There on the steep and narrow single street he had the edifying sight of seeing Tabby, looking very appealing in a short, frilled denim skirt and a white T-shirt, standing chattering and laughing while a grinning tradesman loaded up her van with firewood and admired her lithe, shapely legs. Nowhere could Christien see any evidence that she might have gone shopping to provide him with a breakfast or even that she was anxious to hurry back to the cottage!

Tabby saw the Ferrari and froze in dismay. Christien was watching her from the lowered window, designer sunglasses obscuring his expression, handsome jawline at a determined angle. He swung out of the car, six feet three inches of lean, lithe, gorgeous masculinity. A surge of colour warming her complexion, her mouth running dry as she remembered the passion of the night hours, she watched him approach. 'How did you know where I was?' she asked breathlessly.

'I didn't. I'm on my way home to Duvernay,' Christien murmured smooth as glass.

Tabby looked snubbed.

Against his own volition, Christien found himself smiling. 'I'll pick you up at twelve…OK?'

Warmth and animation leapt back into her expressive face. 'Where are we going?'

'I'd like that to be a surprise, *chérie*.'

When Tabby ought to have been cleaning the ancient kitchen range and scrubbing the terracotta floor tiles, she was washing her hair, daydreaming like a schoolgirl and dampening the single dress she had brought with her in the hope of getting the creases out of it.

Startlingly handsome in tailored cream chinos and a black shirt, Christien collected her and took her to an airfield where they boarded a small private plane.

'*You're* planning to fly us?' Tabby exclaimed in dismay.

'I've had my licence since I was a teenager...I do own an airline,' Christien reminded her gently.

'I don't like flying and, if I have to fly, I'm probably happiest in a jumbo jet,' Tabby confided with a grimace.

'It's a short flight, *ma belle*.' Christien dealt her a wide, appreciative grin that made her heart skip a beat. 'You have to be the only woman I've ever met who would dream of telling me that she hated flying.'

Undaunted by her nervous tension, he kept up a calm running commentary on the sights that she was too ennervated to take in during the flight. He flew with the same confidence with which he drove very fast cars. They landed at an airfield outside Blois where a chauffeur-driven limousine awaited them.

'Curiosity is killing me,' Tabby admitted. 'Where are you taking me?'

'Be patient,' he urged, linking long, lean fingers lazily with hers.

Some ten minutes later, the limo turned up a steep lane bounded on either side by vineyards and finally came to a halt outside an elegant house built of mellow golden stone and ringed by shaded terraces ornamented with urns of beautiful flowers.

'At least tell me who we're visiting...' Tabby hissed.

As Christien mounted the steps a charismatic smile slashed his lean, strong face. 'We're the only visitors.'

Recalling the astonishing pleasure of that beautiful mouth on hers, Tabby felt dizzy and it was an effort to think again. 'Then...what are we doing here?'

Christien pushed the door wide on a spacious tiled hall. 'I'd appreciate a feminine critique of this place.'

Assuming that the house was for sale, Tabby relaxed, flattered that he should want her opinion, but secretly amused that he should have chosen the inappropriate word, 'critique' for a property that even at first glance seemed to possess every possible advantage. It enjoyed immense privacy, a swimming pool and a hillside setting blessed with panoramic views of the wonderful wooded countryside. The interior was even more impressive. Fascinated, she strolled from room to room. It was an old house that had been renovated with superb style. Rich, warm colour, antique and contemporary furniture melded in a timeless joining. French windows led out to cool stone terraces and finally to one where she was surprised to find a uniformed waiter stationed in apparent readiness to serve them beside a table already set with exquisite china and gleaming crystal glasses.

'Lunch,' Christien explained with the utmost casualness as he pulled out a seat for her occupation. 'I don't know about you but I am very hungry. I usually eat at one.'

Tabby sank down and watched the waiter pour the

wine. 'I thought this house belonged to someone else and you were thinking of buying it.'

A broad shoulder lifted in a fluid shrug. 'No, it's already mine but I've never been here before,' he admitted. 'Property is an excellent investment and I buy most of it through advisors sight unseen.'

'I can't imagine owning a house and not being curious enough to come and see it,' she admitted, reminded more than she liked of the vast material differences between them, something she had airily ignored and refused to consider important when she had first known him.

Over a sublime meal of endive salad followed by delicate lamb cutlets that melted in her mouth and a blackberry tart, Christien entertained her with stories of the rich history of the locality before moving on to describe the beautiful, tranquil water meadows of the Sologne as a nature lover's paradise. It was a hot, sultry afternoon and the sky was a deep, intense blue. Far across the lush valley she could see the fanciful turrets of one of the many châteaux in the area. Only birdsong challenged the silence and it was idyllic.

'You haven't offered a single opinion on this place yet,' Christien commented.

'It's fantastic...you've got to know that.' Tabby nibbled at her lower lip, colour lighting her cheeks as she squirmed on the acknowledgement that her standards might well lie far below his. 'But then, of course...I don't know what you're looking for.'

'What pleases you, *ma belle*.' Christien captured and held her startled upward glance. 'That's all I seek.'

Meeting those rich dark eyes framed by black spiky lashes, she could hardly breathe for the pure bolt of longing that shot through her and tightened her skin over her bones. Almost giddy with the force of her response to him, she took a second or two to register what he had just said.

'What pleases...*me*?' Tabby echoed, uncertain of his meaning.

In a graceful movement, Christien rose upright and stretched out a lean brown hand in invitation. 'Let's take another tour...'

He walked her slowly through the house again, but only on a superficial level was she appreciating the beautiful rooms and the stupendous outlook from every window. Her thoughts were in turmoil. Was he asking her to live with him here in this fabulous house? Why else would he care what pleased her in the property stakes? She sucked in a quivering breath in an effort to steady herself, but a wild burst of joy was thrilling through her.

'You like it here...don't you?' he prompted.

'Who wouldn't?' Tabby was so scared that she had picked him up wrong that she vented a discomfited laugh

'It might be too quiet for some, but it strikes me as the perfect environment for an artist. Peaceful and inspiring,' Christien murmured huskily.

It was little more than twenty-four hours since she had arrived in France. Could her eminently sensible and practical Christien be so impulsive? Could he have decided so quickly that he wanted to recapture what they had shared almost four years earlier? Did he, like her, feel bitter at the events that had driven them apart? Was he as greedy as she was to make up for lost time?

Tabby focused on the bottle of champagne in the ice bucket sitting on an occasional table and belatedly took note of the reality that he had chosen to stage the dialogue in the main bedroom. Coincidence? She didn't think so. She tried not to smile at how he planned even romantic gestures for she did not want to offend his pride. At seventeen she had once told him angrily that he had no romance in his soul at all and he had made extraordinary efforts to prove her wrong with surprise gifts and flowers and holding hands without anything more physical in mind. But she had always recognised the cold-blooded, purposeful planning it took for him to make an effort to do anything he saw as an essential waste of time.

'This property is also very convenient to Paris where I spend most of my working week.' As if to stress that leading declaration, Christien drew her back against his lean, muscular length.

The heat and proximity of his lithe, masculine frame tightened her nipples into stiff little points and stirred a dulled ache between her thighs. Trembling, she leant back into him for support. It seemed that he had spoken the truth when he'd told her that the manner of his father's death would never have kept him from her. Tears burned behind her eyes, tears of happiness, and her throat constricted. He was being crazily impractical and that was so out of character for him that it could only mean that he still had strong feelings for her.

Tabby stared hard into the mirror across the room that reflected them both: Christien, so straight and tall and serious and beautiful, her own reflection that of a woman so much smaller, decidedly rounder in shape and a great deal more given to smiles. 'This is so romantic...it must have taken loads of planning—'

'You used to say that the essence of real romance was not being able to see the strings that were being pulled to impress you,' Christien interposed.

'So I was too demanding at seventeen, now I give more points for effort and imagination like that lovely meal—'

When he spun her round and looked down at her, a tremor of almost painful awareness ran through her slight figure for she was weak with wanting. 'Do you, *chérie*?' he asked in a roughened undertone. 'Or when you hear what I have to say, will you accuse me of trying to manipulate you?'

'Perhaps I had better hear what you have to say first,' Tabby said breathlessly.

'I brought you here to suggest a very simple arrangement which would answer both our needs. I offer you this house in place of Solange's property...'

Her lips parted company. 'You've got to be kidding me.'

'No, you would be doing me a favour. A straight swop. Nothing as tasteless as money need change hands. I would prefer not to cut a business deal with you.' His brilliant dark golden eyes urged her to smile at that teasing assurance.

But Tabby had never felt less like smiling. She was also far too busy schooling her features not to betray how much he had wounded her and how bitter was the sting as her own foolish, extravagant hopes crashed and burned. His great-aunt's cottage in exchange for a luxury home five times its size and possessed of every opulent expensive extra? He wanted her off the Duvernay estate very, very badly. After the night she had spent in his arms, that continuing determination felt like a hard, humiliating slap in the face.

'I'd like to leave now.' Her green eyes shiny as polished glass in her determination to show no weakness or emotion, Tabby walked out of the bedroom into the hall. 'I still have so much to do back at the cottage. I have to return to England for a week tomorrow.'

Christien frowned, for she could not hide her sudden pallor. 'Tabby—'

'No, don't say any more or I'll lose my temper,' she warned not quite steadily. 'After all, you brought me here on false pretences and I'm not under any obligation to discuss ridiculous swops or business deals if I don't want to.'

'I did not say you were, but a fair and generous proposition rarely causes offence and usually deserves consideration. I hoped you'd be sensible.'

'And if I'm not, what then? Threats?'

'I don't threaten women,' Christien contradicted with icy disdain. 'You're being irrational. I want to keep the family estate intact and there is no shame in that objective. Nothing that happens between us will change that reality and I won't pretend otherwise.'

Rigid-backed, Tabby stepped out into the hot, still air and headed for the limousine, for she was desperate to be gone. Irrational? Was it irrational to feel unbearably hurt? Was her very presence within miles of the fancy château where he had been born such an offence? She felt sick at her own stupidity. Like a moth to a candle flame she had been drawn to him again. He had burned her before and after that warning it had been very naive of her to invite such pain a second time. But she was angry with him, so angry that she could barely bring herself to look at him and certainly not to speak.

Two hours later, he brought the Ferrari to a halt beside the cottage. As Tabby leapt out he followed suit at a slower pace. 'We have to talk this out,' he drawled with cool determination.

Two high spots of colour burning over her cheek-bones, Tabby shot him a splintering glance. 'No, I don't want to talk to a guy who thinks of me as being something less than he is!'

'You have no grounds to accuse me of that.'

'Oh, haven't I?' A rather shrill laugh fell from her lips. 'You just tried to bribe me…you just tried to *buy* me!'

'It wasn't a bribe. In no way is that house I showed you intended as a bribe. But if I'm asking you to re-think your plans and relocate purely for my benefit, I must offer some form of compensation to make the inconvenience seem worth your while,' Christien pro-claimed without hesitation.

'You are *so* smooth! How is it that you manage to make even the unacceptable sound acceptable?' Tabby demanded with furious resentment.

'I doubt that you would be reacting like this if I had not shared your bed last night. That has clouded the real issue at stake here.' Wide, sensual mouth com-pressing, Christien dealt her a brooding masculine scru-tiny.

'You're right…*that* was a very big mistake.' Tabby slammed the front door loudly shut in his startled face and leant back against it in a tempest of angry, hurting tears.

'Tabby!'

As he rapped on the door she sucked in a steadying breath, but silent, stinging tears trekked down her quiv-ering cheeks. In letting him stay the night she had re-gressed to the impulsive, reckless teenage years. She had forgotten all caution and common sense and flung her heart back at his feet. Did she never learn? Why was she so downright stupid around him?

Sean called her on her mobile phone at seven. The day before he had mentioned knowing the Englishwoman who owned the local art gallery and her daughter, who was a potter.

'Alice has asked us over for drinks. There'll be a crowd, there always is. You're sure to meet a few other creative types,' Sean told her cheerfully.

Tabby felt that company would distract her troubled thoughts from Christien and, although she went out with no expectation of enjoyment, she had an interesting evening. She met several artists living in the area, exchanged phone numbers and garnered useful information about where to buy art supplies. It was two in the morning when Sean brought her home. Only when she saw the lights flick on did she realise that Christien's Ferrari was parked at the side of the cottage. He climbed out, his long, powerful stride carrying him towards her at speed.

Tabby was very tense but determined to save what face she could and she moved forward with as easy and meaningless a smile as she could contrive. 'Christien…sorry I'm so late back—'

'*Zut alors*…I'm not!' he bit out, lean, dark handsome features taut with a scorching fury that took her aback. 'You almost had me convinced that I had misjudged you, but I've caught you in the act again. Where have you been all evening? In his bed? First one man, then another. You sleep with me and—'

'*Regret it,*' Tabby slotted in between angrily clenched teeth. 'Oh, boy, do I regret sleeping with you!'

Appreciating that he had been totally overlooked in the excitement, Sean peered out of his car, which was still parked by the roadside. 'Do you want me to stay, Tabby?' he called anxiously.

'See how you embarrass me!' Tabby snapped at Christien before she stalked back down the path to urge Sean to go on home and not worry about her.

Christien spread lean hands and swore in fast, furious French, demonstrating all the lack of tolerance typical of a male who had never in his whole charmed life been accused of causing anyone embarrassment.

Tabby unlocked the front door with a trembling hand. 'I don't ever want to see you again—'

'Why did you refuse to let me in when I brought you back from viewing the house earlier? You must have known that I would return here.' Christien stepped past her and then swung round to treat her to a fierce look of condemnation. 'Were you scared you might want to spend two nights with the same guy?'

In the moonlight, Tabby shivered with outrage. 'How can you talk to me as if I'm some slapper who goes with a load of different men?'

'When I'm around there's always another guy panting at your heels!'

'Just to think that your friend, Veronique, once told me that *you* liked competition!' Tabby recalled with bitter amusement. 'I guess that piece of misinformation was advanced with the same self-serving venom as all the other helpful advice she offered me.'

Christien had fallen very still. '*Ça alors!* Veronique would never have said such a nonsensical thing—'

'Oh, wouldn't she? Your childhood playmate probably dug out her calculator in that cradle beside yours, worked out what a catch you were and decided right there and then that only she was going to profit. Who knows...who cares?' Tabby was mortified that she had let that petty bitterness out and paraded it for him to see. 'Obviously she knew you had a jealous streak a mile wide and 'guessed that nothing would kill our relationship faster—'

Febrile colour lying along his superb cheekbones, Christien threw back his broad shoulders and studied her with grim disfavour. 'It shames me to lose my temper as I just have and throw allegations that I cannot substantiate *but* I don't trust you—'

Tabby tilted her chin. 'And I won't stand for you accusing me of carrying on with other blokes.'

Eyes glittering gold with anger, Christien vented a harsh laugh. 'What do you expect me to think when you stay out this late and show up with another man in tow?'

'It amazes me that you can even ask me that when I'm the one who has never, ever had the luxury of knowing where I stand with you…yet you are *so* good at criticising my behaviour,' Tabby condemned with a slow, wondering shake of her head. 'Four years ago, you had another woman in your life called Eloise and you never once mentioned her existence to me. You got away with it too, because I was too scared to ask awkward questions—'

His lean, strong face was rigid. 'The minute I saw you it was over with Eloise and it was only a casual thing with her. I ended it soon after I met you. I don't know how you found out about her, but you only had to ask me. Unlike you, I would have been *honest*—'

Savaged by that reminder of her past dishonesty, Tabby twisted away from him and switched on the light. 'So I lied about my age and you know why, but that doesn't mean I can't be trusted—'

'No?'

'No…any more than it excuses you for implying that I'm a tart,' Tabby told him with spirit.

'Where were you until this hour?'

'I'm not telling you, I'm not answering your questions—'

'*Zut alors…*' Christien growled, raking long, lean, impatient fingers through the black silk luxuriance of his hair. 'What do you expect from me?'

Tabby was amazed that in spite of all she had already said he still had no idea whatsoever. 'Respect.'

Christien threw up his expressive hands, studied her with fulminating dark golden eyes, but, while he looked as though he could hardly wait to exercise his sardonic tongue on that ambitious request of hers, he stayed silent.

'Respect,' Tabby repeated doggedly. 'You made a mistake when you decided that I was cheating on you with that boy, Pete, that summer and you owe me an apology.'

'I…*do*?' Burnished dark eyes flared down into hers and she could literally feel the hum of his fierce pride threatening to blow the lid back off his temper again.

'Particularly for the way you treated me at the accident enquiry…I deserved better. You think about that—'

'*Tu parles…*the hell I will!' Christien raked at her and then, as though as disconcerted by that raw outburst as she was, he swung away.

'So that's respect and an apology,' Tabby listed in reminder, deciding to go for gold in the demand stakes. 'But if you want houseroom in my life, I want other stuff too…and I'm not sure if you could make the grade.'

Involuntarily, Christien almost grinned, wondering if

she thought she could train him with her version of 'the carrot and the stick' routine. 'I score very high between the sheets, *ma belle*,' he breathed with husky insolence.

'But unfortunately an awful lot of life takes place outside the bedroom door and offering me a millionaire's residence in place of a tiny cottage was the last straw. Even though I've told you how I feel, you can't respect your great-aunt's wishes or my right to live where I choose,' Tabby spelt out, a great weariness enfolding her, for the stress of the past forty-eight hours and the lack of rest had drained her of her usual highwire energy.

'But—'

'All I want to do right now is jump off my soapbox, fall into bed and sleep like a log,' Tabby cut in heavily.

Christien bent down and swept her up into his arms to carry her upstairs. 'As I wouldn't like you to risk jumping, your wish is my command.'

'Put me down…' Tabby protested in weary frustration, so tired that she was very close to tears.

Christien settled her down on the bed and switched on the lamp. 'Possibly *I* was more at home in the millionaire's residence,' he remarked in a thoughtful concession. 'But you liked it too…don't lie.'

Tabby groaned and let her shoes slide off and drop to the floor. She could not be bothered arguing with him and she let her heavy eyes drift shut. Just to refresh herself for a moment, she promised herself.

Christien gazed down at Tabby while she slept, and sighed. He unbuttoned her shirt and eased it off and removed her skirt. He studied the creamy swell of her breasts above her bra and the incredible peach bloom of her skin and suppressed a groan at his own lack of self-discipline. He wanted to get into bed with her. In fact the intensity of his own desire to be with her even when sex was out of the question unnerved him. He tugged the sheet up over her, put out the light and frowned at the uncurtained window and the front door that lacked any form of proper security. A grim look of disapproval crossed his lean, strong face. He knew that he had decisions to make.

CHAPTER FIVE

'LET me understand this...' Nine hours later, Veronique Giraud studied Christien across the depth of her opulent riverside apartment in Paris. 'You want to break off our engagement for unspecified reasons?'

'Not unspecified. I've come to recognise that I'm not yet ready to commit to a marriage.' Christien's level dark gaze was filled with sincere regret as he surveyed his fiancée in her tailored business suit. 'I only wish that for your sake I had seen that reality sooner.'

'We haven't set a wedding date and I wasn't expecting to set one in the near future,' Veronique pointed out with admirable calm. 'You can take all the time you require to think this decision over.'

Relieved by her unemotional response, Christien expelled his breath. 'I appreciate that but I've had all the time I need to consider this and I must still ask you to release me from our engagement. I'm sorry that it has to be like this.'

After a moment of thought, Veronique gave a gracious nod of acceptance. 'There's no need for you to apologise. I wouldn't want to hold you to our agreement against your will.'

A warm smile of appreciation lightened Christien's grave aspect. 'I know you would never do that. We might have become engaged on a business and social basis but we have a strong friendship as well. I would hate to lose a friendship which I have always valued.

But I will understand if you prefer to let that connection wane now.'

'I wouldn't dream of behaving that way. I won't pretend that I agree with the decision that you've reached, but neither will I make a fuss about it,' the self-contained brunette said briskly. 'However, I hope you won't be annoyed by my frank speech when I say that you will soon discover once again that that little madam is much more trouble than she is worth!'

Almost imperceptibly, Christien tensed. 'You can always be frank with me.'

'Even though I am saying things you cannot possibly want to hear?' Veronique's pale blue eyes had a hard sparkle new to his experience and his keen gaze narrowed.

'Even then.'

'Of course, I know it's the English girl again and I don't want to be crude, but why can't you just scratch the sexual itch and leave it at that level?' Veronique demanded in cold exasperation. 'I assure you that I require no confessions.'

Christien had to make an effort to conceal his distaste. 'Nothing is that simple.'

'But it *is*. It is you who are making it complex by being too conventional and expecting too much of yourself. What has come over you?' the brunette prompted with an air of concerned incomprehension. 'You yourself believe that your parents' relationship was unhealthily obsessive and your mother is *still* unable to function without your father. I understood that you wanted to guard against the risk of making such a destructive marriage—'

'I am not thinking of marriage,' Christien interposed in flat denial.

Veronique looked mollified by that assurance. 'Then why end our engagement over something as trivial as an affair? Fidelity means nothing to me. I don't mind if you keep the Burnside woman as a mistress, for there are far more important matters in life!' she proclaimed with unhidden impatience. 'This situation is exactly why I offered to deal with that calculating little creature on your behalf.'

'Forgive me, but I will not discuss Tabby with you, nor listen to abuse of her.' His brooding dark eyes were veiled, his well-modulated speaking tone discouraging.

Veronique removed the huge solitaire on her engagement finger and set it down on the table with just the suspicion of a snap.

'It is yours…it was a gift,' Christien asserted. 'If you no longer want it, give it to charity.'

Veronique's thin lips stretched into an unexpectedly warm and reassuring smile. Rising, she tucked a slender hand into his elbow. 'At least I can now talk to you as a friend and perhaps you will listen with more patience. I *do* hope that we're still going out to meet our friends for lunch…'

'*So*,' Pippa Stevenson recapped, rolling her very blue eyes, 'although we've moved on nearly four years in our lives you're still happily falling for the Christien Laroche solid gold seduction routine.'

Tabby winced. 'It wasn't like that, Pip—'

'Lean, mean and magnificent, the guy most likely to succeed in business, in bed and every other place because conscience will never keep him awake,' her friend quipped with a cynically curled lip. 'You moving into Christien's neighbourhood is like a goldfish opting to go swimming with sharks!'

Tabby stiffened for, having let herself down very badly, as she felt, with Christien, she was less laid-back about the prospect of taking up permanent residence in the same locality. It was ironic that their renewed intimacy was likely to bring about the sale that he had wanted from the outset, she reflected unhappily. 'I may have to reconsider where Jake and I should live—'

'Considering your non-existent ability to resist Christien, I think that has to be the best news I've heard in a long time!' As Tabby flinched the redhead groaned in guilty embarrassment. 'I'm sorry…I am *truly* sorry. Believe it or not, I didn't invite you and Jake to stay here on your last night in England just so that I could make snide comments.'

'For goodness' sake, I know you didn't…' But as usual, Tabby recognised, her closest friend, who was burdened by a demanding job and the care of a disabled parent, was stressed out and exhausted.

'Whatever happens, I still feel that you ought to tell Christien that he has a son,' Pippa admitted in some discomfiture.

'I agree.' Tabby no longer required prompting on that score. Having reached that same conclusion, she almost smiled at her companion's surprise over her change of heart. 'When I decided to move to Brittany, I honestly did believe that I wouldn't see Christien again. I didn't think things through, which was foolish and short-sighted—'

'Easy enough to do in the circumstances.' Pippa gave her a look of understanding.

'But I *do* think it would be unfair to put Christien in an awkward position with his family…or perhaps a girlfriend over Jake while we're living so close,' Tabby revealed uneasily. 'I still have to work out how best to handle that.'

'It's Christien's own fault that he's likely to be the last to know about Jake. Naturally you were intimidated by the animosity that you met with when you attended the inquest into the crash.' Pippa frowned. 'That was so cruel—'

'But the way some people couldn't help feeling and probably will *still* feel about me,' Tabby emphasised with a grimace. Pippa dropped her gaze and neither woman chose to mention the reality that, since that accident, Tabby had also lost touch with their other friends, Hilary and Jen.

'They needed a focus for their bitterness and grief and Dad was dead, so I made the next best target,' Tabby continued. 'It's just I couldn't bear Christien or anybody else in his family to look at Jake in that same tainted light…as though he was something to be ashamed of, apologised for and concealed—'

'Why should he be? Your son is the mirror image of his very handsome papa. And Christien Laroche is not the male I took him for if he does not relish the sight of himself reprised in miniature,' Pippa opined drily. 'Furthermore, when Jake reveals his meteoric IQ and his deeply boring current obsession with fast cars Christien will experience such a shocking sense of soul-deep recognition that he will be flattered to death.'

Tabby cherished much less ambitious notions. She only hoped that once Christien got over the shock, he would be interested in getting to know his son. An hour later, sighing at the sound of her much-put-upon friend trekking downstairs again to fulfil yet another late-night demand from her domineering parent, Tabby climbed into the spare-room bed where Jake already lay fast asleep.

Eight days had passed since she had left France. Christien had tucked her into bed that last night and left her alone. Although that was what she had wanted, she had felt ridiculously abandoned the next morning and very sad driving away in the van. Indeed it had been a week during which Tabby had become increasingly angry with herself for her repeated failure to push Christien out of her mind, not to mention her reluctance to tell Christien that he was the father of her child. That smacked of a cowardice that Tabby was determined to confront within herself.

As Tabby drove off the ferry into France the following day she was keen to draw Jake's attention to the more unusual cars on the road to keep him occupied during the lengthy drive ahead. 'There's a Rolls Royce...' she told her son helpfully.

The little boy shifted excitedly in his seat.

'Are you excited about the new house?' Tabby asked.

'Can I jump on my new bed?'

'Forget it!' Tabby said with a grin.

The minute Tabby parked in the driveway at the cottage, Jake headed straight for the back garden with his football, eager to stretch his legs after being cooped up for so long. Tabby decided to let him burn off some energy before she took him indoors. In truth, she was afraid of seeing disappointment on his earnest little face. He was only three years old and it took adult imagination to see that the drab cottage had promise.

'Stay in the garden and don't go near the road!' she

called in his wake, knowing her first priority would have to be the installation of a gate across the driveway.

Jake stopped and uttered a world-weary sigh that would have done justice to a little old man. 'I *know*...I'm not a baby now,' he muttered in reproach.

Entering the cottage while she thought about how shockingly fast Jake seemed to be growing up, Tabby came to an abrupt halt and stared with bewildered eyes at her unfamiliar surroundings. In panic she started backing outside again, believing that she had somehow contrived to gain entry to someone else's home. Only when she saw the gorgeous artistic arrangement of flowers beside the fireplace and the large envelope that bore her name in Christien's writing did she halt her retreat. In a daze, Tabby crept back inside again and snatched up the envelope to extract the card within.

'I respect your right to live where you choose...call me, Christien.'

A phone sat beside the floral offering. He had even had a phone line connected. The windows had been replaced and the walls had been painted in fresh colours. In a daze she looked around the room, which now was furnished with twin sofas and a handsome *armoire*. Dumbstruck, she peered into the kitchen and saw superb new freestanding units complete with discreet appliances and a beautiful dining set. A clock ticked on the mantel. The wine rack was packed with bottles. She looked into a fridge bursting with fresh produce and let the door fall shut again. Her son waved at her from the garden and she lifted a nerveless hand in response.

All of a tremble, she snatched up the phone and stabbed out the number that Christien had put on the card. As she waited for the call to connect she glanced into the little washroom and stopped dead. Because the 'little' washroom now appeared to encompass the enclosed porch beyond it as well and had a shower, marble tiles and a Jacuzzi that was state-of-the-art. A walkin airing cupboard was packed with an array of fleecy towels and what looked very much like entire rows of crisp bed linen.

'Tabby...what do you think?' Christien purred as she hurried up the stairs with the receiver of the cordless phone clutched in her perspiring hand.

'I think...I think I'm hallucinating,' she mumbled, gaping at the rich wool carpet on the stairs.

'*Bien*...I thought I was having a nightmare when I first saw inside the cottage as it was,' Christien confided teasingly. 'A home fit only for a cave dweller—'

'Christien...there is just no way that I can accept any of this,' Tabby asserted in a wobbly voice. 'Have you gone out of your mind? This whole place has been torn apart and remodelled into far more than it was ever meant to be. It's so seriously trendy it must have cost a fortune!'

'It's my way of saying sorry for being pushy and welcoming you back to your new home, *ma belle*,' Christien murmured smoothly.

'How on earth did you even get into this place?' Tabby queried. 'Did you break in?'

Her bedroom had been embellished with a bed in which a princess would have felt at home and dressed with snazzy silk curtains and an over abundance of crisp white lace-edged pillows and sheets. The colour scheme was in her favourite shades of pale turquoise and lemon and she wondered dizzily if he had remembered that.

'Solange kept a spare key hidden in the trunk of the

old tree in the front garden. I've removed it,' he confessed.

'Thanks for warning me!' Tabby sniped, but the reproof lacked bite because her voice was weak. 'I just can't believe you've done all this…and in such an incredibly short space of time.' She glanced into Jake's room, which, having already been furnished, had benefited a little less noticeably from fresh paint and polished floorboards. 'What are you expecting in return? Me in a gift box?'

His husky, sexy laugh vibrated down her spinal cord like a caress.

'How am I supposed to hand back new windows when you haven't left me the old ones?' Tabby demanded, looking out the bedroom window to note that a big glossy car had stopped out on the quiet road.

'When I want you to climb into a gift box for me, you can be sure I'll cut off all avenues of retreat—'

'But I can't accept a generosity that I can't match—'

'Are you discriminating against me because I'm rich?' Christien countered with mockery.

Tabby walked downstairs again. 'If I accepted all this stuff…well, it would make me feel like I'm in your power—'

'That works fine for me,' Christien slotted in without shame.

'Or like I owed you big time—'

'I can't say that that idea turns me off either. I know it's not politically correct but, if your conscience is heavy, I could give you a suggestion or two on how best to lighten—'

'Shut up!' But Tabby was laughing until she went over to the kitchen window to check on Jake, only to discover he was nowhere within view. 'Hold on a minute,' she urged Christien then. 'Look, I'll call you back!'

After distractedly pressing the 'hold' button, then discarding the phone, Tabby headed into the front garden. Relieved that Jake had not strayed round there as she had feared, she took the time to study the car still sitting parked because she couldn't help wondering what it was doing there. It was a Mercedes and a very expensive-looking model. She was heading for the side of the cottage where she assumed her son was playing when she saw Jake running out from behind the van. He was chasing his ball, which was bouncing down the sloping driveway towards the road.

'No, Jake…*stop!*' Tabby screamed at the top of her voice.

But her shout was drowned out as the engine of the Mercedes suddenly ignited and the vehicle moved off. Even knowing that she was too far away, Tabby made a frantic attempt to reach her son and prevent him from running out into the road in front of the car. But she was too late. With a protesting screech of tyres, the driver braked hard and swerved to avoid Jake and the Mercedes mounted the verge with a crashing jolt before coming to a juddering halt.

For a split second deafening silence held and then Jake broke it with a frightened howl. Tabby grabbed him up, sat him down on the driveway and told him firmly to stay there while she raced across the road to check on the driver. The car door fell open and a slender, middle-aged blonde lurched out, her white face a mask of shock.

'Are you hurt?' Tabby gasped and then, fumbling for the French words, used them as well.

The woman hovered at the side of the road and

stared fixedly at Jake. Then she began to sob noisily. Curving a supportive arm round her and feeling quite sick herself at what had so nearly transpired, Tabby urged the woman indoors. She offered to call a doctor and when that suggestion was met with a dismayed frown asked if the lady would like to call anyone. That too was met with a silent negative and she was careful to apologise for having left Jake alone in the garden.

'It was not your fault. Children will be children,' the woman finally responded in English while she continued to study Jake as if not yet fully convinced that he was wholly unharmed. 'We must thank *le bon Dieu* that he is safe. He is…your son? May I ask what he is called?'

'I'm Jake. Jake…Christien…Burnside,' Jake recited with care.

The lady was trembling. She twisted her head away and fumbled for another tissue from the box that Tabby had set beside her, her thin hands shredding at it as she choked back another sob.

'You're in shock and I'm not surprised after the fright my son must have given you,' Tabby said worriedly. 'Are you sure I can't phone the doctor for you, *madame*?'

'Perhaps…if I could have a glass of water?' The woman snatched in a deep breath in a clear effort to calm herself.

'Of course.' Tabby returned with the glass and found Jake chattering about cars and holding the woman's beringed hand. Tabby introduced herself.

A strange little silence fell

'Ma-Manette,' the older woman finally stammered, suddenly awkward again, her reddened eyes lowering.

'Manette…eh, Bonnard. Your son is so sweet. He kissed me because he saw that I was sad.'

Tabby took the opportunity to explain to Jake why Madame Bonnard had been sad and why he must never, ever again run out into a road.

'Please don't scold Jake…I am sure he will be more careful in the future.' Although Manette Bonnard was smiling and it seemed a very genuine smile, her eyes still glistened with unshed tears.

'Do you have a little boy like me?' Jake asked.

'A big boy,' their visitor answered.

'Does he like cars?'

'Very much.'

'Is he taller than me?' Perceptibly, Jake was stretching himself up, his innate competitive streak in the ascendant, dark brown eyes sparkling.

'Yes. He is all grown up,' Manette Bonnard said apologetically.

'Is he a good boy?'

'Not all the time.'

'I'll be very tall and very good when I get grown up,' Jake informed her confidently.

Keen to see the older woman fully recovered before she got back into her car, Tabby offered her coffee. A rather dazed look etched in her fine dark eyes, their visitor nodded polite acceptance while trying to answer Jake's questions. Jake had no inhibitions about being nosy and, by dint of simply listening to the older woman's initially hesitant replies, Tabby learned that their guest lived in Paris in an apartment that had *twelve* bedrooms and also had a summer home in the area.

'Mummy…can I show Madam Bonnard one of your pictures?' Jake pleaded.

'If it would not be too much of an intrusion, *mademoiselle*,' Manette Bonnard interposed. 'I collect miniatures.'

Tabby got her first glimpse of the sun lounge since her return and discovered that in Christien's makeover even her studio had gained sleek storage units and a wonderful mosaic tiled floor. The older woman enthused at length over the two tiny canvases she was shown and was disappointed to learn that both were earmarked for a client.

'I must not take up any more of your time, *mademoiselle*,' their visitor finally sighed with regret.

'I like you,' Jake told Madame Bonnard.

Tabby was unsurprised that Jake was so taken with the older woman for Manette Bonnard had demonstrated flattering enthusiasm for her son's company and had made no attempt to hide her appreciation from him. But she was dismayed when their very emotional visitor looked as though she was about to go off into floods of tears again.

'Are you sure that you feel well enough to drive?' Tabby prompted with concern.

The older woman kept her head down and patted Tabby's hand in an uncertain but apologetic gesture. 'Please don't worry…you don't understand…I am sorry,' she muttered in confusion before she broke away to hurry across the road and take refuge in her car.

Tabby was relieved to see that the Mercedes drove off at a slow speed.

She darted back indoors intending to ring Christien back and then she fell still, the excitement in her discomfited eyes dwindling. Why did Christien always do what she least expected? She had been angry and hurt when she'd last seen him and she had believed that she could forget their night of passion and write it off as the result of her own foolishness. His arrogant assumption that he could make her do what she did not want to do had offended and mortified her and persuaded her that it was not possible for her to try to rewrite the past with Christien. But in the space of a week, Christien had turned all her expectations upside down.

He had gone to extraordinary lengths to demonstrate that he had accepted her right to live in Solange Laroche's cottage. He had transformed the humble little dwelling into a sophisticated and trendy property bristling with luxury extras. Of course, he had had no right to do that, but it scarcely mattered now, did it? After all, if she was planning to seek a permanent home elsewhere, she would be selling the cottage back to Christien and it would have to be at a price that did not take account of the improvements that he had made at his own expense.

In retrospect her own weakness with Christien seemed unforgivable and inexcusable. She had not told him about Jake. She had let her heart and her hormones carry her away and she had slept with him again. The Jacuzzi big enough for two suggested that Christien was very keen to repeat that experience. Only Christien had no idea at all that she was the mother of a three-year-old, who had already contrived to leave a muddy footprint on one of the slinky cream sofas. And she was not just any single parent either, she was the mother of *his* child. How was she to break that news to him? Especially with Jake under the same roof? She gathered Jake into a hug and rested her chin down into his dark silky curls. Her eyes were stinging.

'Our clothes are in the van,' her son reminded her. 'We'll go out and get our cases.'

Having fetched their luggage in, Tabby called Christien back.

'Why did you leave me on hold?' he demanded.

'I didn't…I must have pushed the button wrong,' she answered, her voice a little thick.

'I was worried that some disaster had occurred… What are we doing tonight?'

He was the only guy she had ever met whose voice could make her melt like ice on a griddle. 'Would you come here? About eight?'

'Do I have to wait three hours?' he groaned.

'Yeah…sorry.' She wanted Jake in bed and safely asleep before Christien arrived.

'We'll dine out—'

'Eat before you get here,' Tabby advised tensely.

'*Eat?* Before eight in the evening?' Christien demanded in disbelief.

'Stop being so French. I…I've got something serious I need to discuss with you.'

There was a short, intense silence.

'So have I…the outrageous concept of dining before eight and being told to feed myself when I've offered to feed you,' Christien quipped.

'I'll see you then…' Tabby drew in a slow, deep, steady breath and finished the call.

She unpacked one suitcase, two boxes of Jake's toys, bathed her son in the Jacuzzi and watched him fall asleep over the simple supper that she made. She carried him up to bed and tucked him in before taking a quick shower. Then she trawled through two more suitcases before she found the casual khaki skirt and white camisole top she wanted to wear. She put on make-up, which she usually didn't bother with. She wondered why she *was* bothering when the very last thing Christien was likely to be doing after she broke the news about Jake was notice her appearance.

A bag of nerves at the prospect of the confrontation that lay ahead, Tabby paced the floor. She froze when she heard his powerful sports car pulling up outside. Way beyond any concept of playing it cool, she opened the door and watched him stride towards her: a breathtakingly good-looking guy in a lightweight pearl-grey designer suit.

Christien sent her a slashing smile that had a devastating effect on her defences. 'I'm not stupid, *ma belle*. I've worked it out. You think you're pregnant!'

CHAPTER SIX

TRANSFIXED by that charge, Tabby stared at him with wide startled green eyes, her dismay unconcealed. 'Er…you think there's a chance of that?'

'I didn't take any risks but I do know that accidents happen and you sounded as though you were crying on the phone.' Dark colour now delineating the hard angles of his superb cheekbones, Christien shrugged back his broad shoulders in a dismissive gesture as he read her expressive face. '*Mais non*…I can see that that isn't the "something serious" you referred to.'

'No…er, it wasn't.'

Black brows drew together over his clear dark golden eyes. 'You're ill?' he breathed in a roughened undertone.

'Healthy as a horse.'

'Then we've got nothing at all to worry about, *mon ange*.' Thrusting the door shut in his wake and without skipping a beat, Christien curved his hands round her slight, taut shoulders and pulled her to him.

Tabby snatched in a short, sharp gasp of air. '*Christien*—'

'Don't cry wolf with me. I was really concerned.' But there was no true anger in his accented drawl for when she was that close he believed that he could have forgiven her anything short of cold-blooded murder.

'I know, but—'

Moulding her slight body to him, he vented a husky groan of very male satisfaction as the surging peaks of

111

her full breasts met the hard, muscular wall of his chest. His hands curved round her bottom to bring her into closer contact with the rigid thrust of his erection.

'*Zut alors*…being with you is *all* I've thought about since you phoned!' Christien dragged in a deep shuddering breath because all he wanted to do at that instant was sate the savage ache of his desire: push her back against the wall, lift her, sink into her over and over again. No more finesse than an animal, he acknowledged in shock at himself.

Weak with the same overwhelming hunger, Tabby trembled, awash with wild, mindless response to him on a half-dozen different levels. Fighting for the self-control to pull back from his lean, powerful body, she pushed her face into his neck, but the unique scent of his bronzed skin, of *him* was the headiest of aphrodisiacs. Her heart thumping like crazy, she rubbed against him, instinctively seeking relief from the throbbing sensitivity of her nipples.

Swearing barely audibly, Christien knotted long fingers into her hair to tip her head back. Smouldering dark golden eyes blazed down into hers and she stretched up to him as though he had thrown a switch somewhere inside her. He crushed her mouth under his, delved deep with his tongue in an explicit rhythm that made her knees buckle and damp heat pool between her thighs.

'I need to be inside you…' Christien growled and, backing to the sofa, he brought her down on top of him.

When she tensed and made a whimper of sound that just might have been the beginning of an objection, he was too clever to employ reason. Instead he pushed the camisole up out of his path and negotiated the hazard of the stretchy inner lining supporting her breasts. When the plump rosy-tipped mounds tumbled free, he groaned in raw male approbation of their bounty. Cupping the creamy swells, he used his tongue on her stiff, sensitised nipples and she gasped in tormented delight beneath his skilful ministrations.

'We *can't*...' Tabby mumbled in despair, fighting her own unbearable craving with all her might.

Christien hushed her and a sob caught in her throat as he stroked a tantalising finger across the taut wet triangle of fabric stretched between her thighs. 'I *love* your body, I *love* the way you respond to me—'

'I...*have* to talk to you—'

'I'll be much more receptive in an hour's time when I've recovered from nine days of deprivation,' Christien promised huskily.

Already he had her so excited she couldn't get oxygen into her lungs. He was touching her and she was lost in the ever-building flow of sweet, seductive sensation. Clutching his shoulders for support, she let her head fall back, helpless while he toyed with her.

'Tell me how much you missed me, *ma belle*,' he urged against her lush, reddened mouth, but she was way beyond speech. Her whole being was concentrated on the wicked joy of what he was doing to her.

At a fever pitch of desire, she was quivering all over. Heart racing, she gyrated against his expert hand, crazy with hunger as the throbbing ache at the heart of her drove her on with shameless eagerness. Knotting one hand into her tumbling hair, he plunged his tongue into her readily opened mouth, once, twice with explicit, erotic force...and it was enough to push her over the edge into a shattering release that wrenched a cry of ecstasy from her.

Only as the wild tremors of her climax and the mist of mindless pleasure receded did Tabby become aware of her mortal body again. He held her close, murmuring soothing, incomprehensible things in French as if he knew that, both emotionally and physically, he had turned her inside out. He tipped her back from him, smoothing her tangled hair back from her brow.

He sent her a slashing smile that made her heart lurch. 'Although you couldn't tell me that I was missed, you can certainly *show* me,' he murmured with wicked appreciation.

Tabby reddened to the roots of her hair. He was still fully clothed. She had been so out of it that the pleasure had been hers alone. In a clumsy movement, her face burning with shame and embarrassment at how out of control she had been, she scrambled off his lap and pulled her camisole down from her bare breasts. While she stood there trembling from shock at what had happened to her in his arms, lean bronzed hands smoothed down her rucked skirt and then enclosed her clenched fingers.

Slowly, Christien turned her back round to face him. 'Your passion gives me a hell of a kick. Don't you know how rare it is? I don't want a woman who worries about creasing her clothes or wrecking her hair—'

'Basically, you're happiest with a trollop!' Tabby framed in a wobbly voice, and then she literally fled to the bathroom before she let herself down even more and burst into tears.

Even there she got no privacy. Christien opened the door a crack. 'We'll go out to dinner and lust over each other throughout at least five courses...will that make you feel better?'

A hairbrush gripped between her fingers, Tabby

looked at her shameful reflection in the mirror and
knew that nothing was likely to make her feel better.
'We can't go out...I have to tell you something...and
you're going to hate me.'

Silence fell and grew thick and heavy outside the
bathroom door.

'Is there another guy involved?' Christien enquired
roughly.

'No.'

'No problem...there's nothing else I can't handle.
I'm very shock-proof,' Christien asserted with complete confidence. 'Do we *have* to sit through a five-
course dinner? I'm hungry but I'm infinitely hun-
grier...and needier for you.'

Her throat thickened. 'I'll be out in a minute. Open
one of those bottles of wine.'

'You want me to wait upstairs?' A ragged laugh
sounded from Christien. 'If I sound desperate, it's because I am. I'm in agony!'

'Just stay downstairs,' Tabby instructed unsteadily.

She shut her eyes tight, forcing back the tears that
would have released her tension. She was convinced
that no woman had ever made a bigger mess of a relationship. She loved him. She had never stopped loving him. She loved just about everything about him:
his sense of humour, his forceful personality, the passion and energy that he brought into every aspect of
his life, even that volatile streak of possessiveness that
was so contrary to his cool façade. But he didn't love
her. He lusted after her like mad and that was the
height of her power over him.

When he'd arrived, she should have kept him at
arm's length, maintained a formal distance that would
have been more conducive to the confession that she

had to make. What she had just done, what she had just allowed him to do to her, had been very unwise and wrong. But then in her own defence she still had no very clear idea of how she had ended up on that sofa with Christien. Any more than there was anything new in her shell-shocked reaction to her own behaviour with him. When Christien touched her, everything but him blurred out of focus and importance. However, this one time, Tabby thought painfully, just this *one* time she should have had enough gumption to stay in control for her son's sake.

'What's worrying you?' Emanating megawatt self-assurance and calm, Christien passed her a glass of wine when she came out of the bathroom, narrowed dark golden eyes intent on her troubled face.

'What's worrying me goes back nearly four years,' Tabby informed him tightly, tipping the wine to her dry lips but barely able to bring herself to swallow.

'You've just come back into my life. It would seem more sensible to leave the past where it belongs for now,' Christien drawled.

'I'm afraid that this is a piece of the past that's not going to go away and roll back up at a more convenient time,' Tabby mumbled and, feeling her knees going weak under her, she sank down on a sofa and stared into her wineglass. 'That summer, do you remember me telling you that I was taking the contraceptive pill?'

Disconcerted by that question, Christien frowned. '*Oui...*'

Tabby was embarrassed and she refused to look at him. 'It was the doctor's idea that I start taking it because I was having problems with my skin...acne. Well, I was given a three-month supply but I lost a packet somewhere, which meant that I ran out of them while I was still in France.'

'Ran out of them…?' Christien queried in bewilderment.

Tabby cringed, for it was hard to admit just how naive she had been in those days. 'I didn't think it mattered too much if I had to miss a couple of weeks. Unfortunately, I had this really stupid idea that the pills had a sort of cumulative effect after they'd been taken for a while.'

'Are you saying…?' Christien breathed in a seriously strained undertone. 'Are you saying that even though you were no longer taking the pills you believed that you would *still* be protected from pregnancy?'

As Christien's tone rose in volume, Tabby flinched. 'Don't shout at me…I know it was stupid, but back then I didn't know anything about stuff like that. When I was put on that course of pills, I didn't need to be interested in the small print because it never occurred to me that I would be relying on them as birth control…I didn't know you were about to come into my life!'

'I don't believe this. Why the hell didn't you ask *me* to take precautions?' Christien raked at her with incredulous bite.

'Well…'

His stubborn jawline clenched. 'I thought you'd be challenged to answer that—'

'No, just embarrassed. You'd told me that you disliked condoms—'

'*Zut alors!*' Christien exclaimed.

'And I didn't want to annoy you and I persuaded myself that there was no real risk.' Tabby loosed a sad, shamefaced sigh. 'I was seventeen and I couldn't imagine falling pregnant. I thought it couldn't happen to me and, of course, it *did*.'

That simple admission lay there like a stone thrown into a deceptively tranquil pond. A pond that was about to start churning up beneath the surface. Pale below his olive skin, Christien stared at her from the other side of the room, magnificent golden eyes shimmering with the ferocity of his tension.

Tabby fixed her discomfited gaze back on her wineglass and then she set it down in an abrupt movement.

'I found out that I was going to have a baby soon after I went back to England...I had morning sickness like...morning, afternoon and evening too,' she recalled in a small, flat voice. 'To cut the wretched long story short, he—'

'*He?*'

'Our son was born three weeks before the inquest into the car crash was held.' Tabby pleated her trembling hands together to keep them steady. 'I intended to tell you then—'

'*Bon Dieu*...why that late in the day? Why didn't I hear that I was to be a father months before that?' Christien shot at her rawly.

'You changed your mobile phone number. I tried to call the villa in the Dordogne but, by that stage, you had sold it and I had no other address or means of contacting you—'

'That's not much of an excuse. You could have made more effort.'

'I didn't have your resources to conduct an all-out search *and* I had other problems!' Tabby's temper was sparking in her own defence. 'In his will, my father left everything he possessed to my stepmother and when she realised I was pregnant she threw me out of the house in literally what I stood up in. I had just started art college and I had to sleep on a friend's floor until my mother's sister, Alison, took me in.'

'I am certain that she could have advised you on the best way to locate me...such as through the name of my airline.' Majoring in heavy sarcasm as he pointed that out, Christien was not yielding an inch.

'I think you're overlooking the fact that you dumped me like a hot potato after that car accident and never spoke to me again—'

'The crash had nothing to do with it. I saw you with that idiot on the Harley—'

'But I didn't know *how* it was with you, did I? I wasn't inside your secretive head with you!' Tabby scanned him with strained eyes that demanded his understanding. 'I wasn't aware that you believed I was seeing someone else. All I knew was that you wanted nothing more to do with me after the death of your father and mine. So you had better believe that I wasn't in any great hurry just then to track you down with the news that I was pregnant...because, believe it or not, I have my pride too!'

Christien was very pale. He raked a not quite steady hand through his luxuriant black hair, his dark eyes brooding and bitter. 'Why don't you just get to the point? So, you gave my son up for adoption!'

Tabby registered that she should have guessed that he would assume that she had put their baby up for adoption. After all, he had seen no sign of a child in her life when he'd visited her in London the previous month or when she'd stayed in the cottage over that first weekend. 'No, I *didn't* do that. I couldn't give him up. He's upstairs fast asleep...'

Black brows pleating, Christien gazed back at her, what she had just revealed too shattering for him to accept. '*Comment?*'

'I called him Jake Christien and your name is on his birth certificate. I planned to tell you about him when I attended the accident enquiry.' Tabby couldn't keep the bitter hurt out of her voice. 'But you wouldn't have anything to do with me—'

'What are you trying to say?' Christien was not focusing on what to him was an irrelevance. 'You are saying that you have our son...that there is a little boy *here* in this house? I don't believe you—'

'The day you visited me in London, he was at nursery school, and I left him in England with Alison when I made my first trip here.' Tabby rose to her feet as she appreciated that she might as well have been talking to a brick wall for all the listening that Christien seemed able to do.

'Right *now*, he is upstairs?' Christien questioned fiercely.

Tabby halted at the foot of the staircase and whispered, 'How...how do you feel about that?'

'That I can't believe that this is real because, if I start believing it, I might get so angry I lose my head with you.' Dark golden eyes glittering, Christien stared at her with deadly seriousness. 'I can't believe it's real because you slept with me last week without saying a word—'

A deep dark blush flamed over her face. 'I didn't mean to—'

He dealt her a derisive glance. 'I want to *see* him—'

'He's asleep...OK.' Intimidated by the anger flaring in his expectant gaze, she went upstairs and crossed the landing to push the door of Jake's room wider open.

Behind her, Christien stilled like a guy turned to stone. A night-light illuminated the bed. Jake seemed to be having a restive night for his little face was flushed, his black curls tousled, the sheet in a tangle round his waist. With strong, determined hands, Christien set Tabby out of his path and entered the room. Her heart leapt into her mouth as she wondered what he planned to do. For long, endless moments, he stared down at Jake and then at the long row of toy cars parked with military exactitude along the skirting board. He released a long, low, shuddering breath and then very slowly began to back out again.

The silence on the landing was so intense that it screamed.

Tabby hurried back downstairs.

Christien drew level with her again and looked at her, searing dark eyes hard with condemnation. 'You're the equivalent of a kidnapper who never asked for a ransom.'

Tabby blanched.

'Once again you lied to me, but this time the consequences were much worse,' he continued with harsh clarity. 'This time, an innocent child has suffered—'

'Jake has not suffered—'

'Of course, he has! He has had no father!' Christien slung back without hesitation. 'Don't try to tell me that that hasn't made a difference to my child's life. Don't try to make some sexist point arguing that a mother figure is more important—'

Caught unprepared by the cutting force of his attack, Tabby was pale as milk. 'I wasn't going to—'

'*Zut alors*...just as well!' Christien snarled. 'Not unless you want to hear how outraged I am at the knowledge that a stupid schoolgirl has been attempting to raise my son!'

'Don't you call me stupid.' Tabby's temper flared. 'I might not be a real brainbox like you, but there's nothing wrong with my brain—'

'*Isn't* there?' Christien incised at the speed of a rapier. 'You've already told me that, until your aunt offered you a bed, you were sleeping on a floor while you were pregnant. Had you contacted me, you would have been living in luxury. So *not* contacting me was an act of inexcusable stupidity!'

'Listening to you right now, not contacting you strikes me as having been a very clever decision. Being a filthy rich, smug four-letter-word doesn't make you any more acceptable!' Tabby shot back at him.

'Except in the parent stakes. Strive to focus on the main issue, *chérie*. Four years ago, it was your responsibility to protect our unborn child by taking no risks with your own health. Since when was sleeping on floors recommended for pregnant women?'

Compressing her lips, Tabby turned her head away.

'But in the present, our primary concern must simply be Jake…*not* how I feel about your lies or how you feel about me. This is about Jake and *his* rights.' Christien lifted a forceful brown hand to stress his point. 'And his most basic right was his father's care, which you chose to deny him.'

Tabby knotted her trembling hands tightly together. Her palms were damp, her eyes felt scratchy and her throat was so tight it was hurting. No matter how hard she attempted to make herself she could not hold Christien's outraged dark golden gaze. It was as if he had got her by the throat and stolen every excuse she might have employed before she even got the chance to think any up. Jake and *his* rights. No, she had to admit that her son's right to know his father had only occurred to her in more recent times when she had had to face the fact that Jake would soon be reaching an age when he would be asking awkward questions.

'The way you felt about me, I didn't think you'd want to know about him.' Tabby knew she sounded accusing, but she could not help it for she did not think it was fair for him to refuse to acknowledge that his treatment of her had naturally influenced her expectations and her opinion of him.

'That decision was not yours to make—'

'OK...I went to the accident enquiry determined to tell you that you were the father of my son but you couldn't even give me five minutes of your time—'

As Tabby made that reminder the angular lines of Christien's fabulous bone structure hardened into prominence below his olive skin, but he stood his ground. 'That is not the point—'

'Excuse me, that is *exactly* the point!' Tabby argued fiercely, recalling the terrible feeling of humiliation she had experienced that day and stiffening in sick remembrance. 'I was ready, willing and eager to tell you about Jake. I think you need to remember what a louse you were to me that day—'

'I did and I said nothing—'

'And nothing was precisely what you deserved and got for treating me like the dirt beneath your feet!' Tabby hurled furiously. 'I practically begged you to speak to me in private in spite of the fact that your awful snobby relatives and friends were all lined up with you and shooting me looks of loathing as if *I*, rather than my father, had been the cause of that ghastly accident!'

Christien was rigid and pale with rage. '*Ciel!* That day I was too busy grieving for my father to concern myself with the behaviour of other people—'

'You didn't give a damn! I was eighteen and I was alone in a foreign country and I was grieving too.' Tabby was shaking, raw with pain and the need to justify her own actions and defend herself. 'But you talk now and you behaved then as if you had cornered the grief market. You lost a father. Well, at least you were able to look back on your memories of him with respect and affection. I was denied even that because my dad got drunk and destroyed a lot of other lives as well as his own!'

Christien spread two lean hands in a movement of angry rebuttal. 'I did not even notice how others were behaving. If you think that grief was all that lay behind my distance with you that day—'

'Don't you shout at me!' Tabby interrupted wrathfully.

Hauling in a furious breath, Christien then froze in bewilderment at the strange noise he could hear emanating down from the floor above. Tabby was quicker to recognise and react to her son's frightened howl and she raced for the stairs in automatic maternal pilot. She found Jake sitting bolt upright in bed, tears running down his pale, scared face.

'The car…the car ran me over!' her son sobbed, letting her work out for herself what had caused the nightmare that had wakened him from his sleep.

Tabby tugged his small, trembling body into her arms. 'It was just a dream, Jake…just a dream. The car didn't run you over. You're safe. You're all right. You got a fright but you weren't hurt,' she told him with a note of soothing and determined cheer in her quiet intonation.

But the consequence that she had feared from the minute she ran to her son's bedside was already happening. Although Jake had stopped crying as soon as she'd put her arms round him, he was now struggling for breath and wheezing. Worse, because he was not yet fully awake and still recovering from the effects of his nightmare, he was all the more distressed by his physical difficulties.

CHAPTER SEVEN

CHRISTIEN was paralysed to the spot by shock as he watched Jake fight to get air into his skinny little chest. As Christien had not even a nodding acquaintance with what fear felt like, his fear on his son's behalf hit him as hard as a bullet from a gun. He watched Tabby grab up what looked like an inhaler and tend to the little boy. *His* little boy.

'What's the matter with him...what can I do?' Christien demanded, sick to the stomach with the force of his concern.

'You don't need to do anything. Jake's fine.' Tabby's squeaky tone was a leaden but obvious attempt to conceal her anxiety sooner than increase the risk of Jake getting more upset. 'It's just a little asthma attack and the medication in the bronchodilator will help put it under control.'

Unimpressed and constitutionally incapable of standing around doing nothing and feeling helpless, Christien stepped out onto the landing, dug out his mobile phone and hastily called a doctor.

Even as his son's breathing difficulties subsided Christien discovered that he could not take his attention from Jake. In appearance the little boy was unmistakably a Laroche. His black curls ran down into a peak at the hairline just as Christien's did. His eyes were just like his paternal grandmother's—dark, liquid and very expressive. His olive skin was in direct contrast to Tabby's fair colouring and the pure lines of his bone structure were already hinting at the strong features that could be seen in the family paintings. However, in apparent defiance of those genes from a tall, well-built family, Jake looked shockingly small and slight to Christien, who had had very little to do with young children. But then illness had probably stunted his son's growth, Christien reflected sadly.

Tabby's tension was beginning to drain away when Christien sat down on the other side of Jake's bed as though it was the most natural thing in the world. Jake stared at the tall, dark male in his city suit with huge surprised eyes.

Tabby was annoyed that Christien was pushing in just when she had got her son calmed down. 'Jake... this is—'

Christien closed a hand over Jake's tiny one and breathed shakily, 'I am your papa...your father, Christien Laroche—'

'Christien!' Tabby hissed in a piercing whisper, shaken by the ill-considered immediacy of that startling announcement. 'If you upset him, it could cause another—'

'Daddy...?'

Jake was studying Christien with big, wondering eyes.

'Daddy...Papa. You can call me whatever you like.' Satisfied to have introduced himself and claimed his rightful place in his son's life, Christien smoothed a thumb over the little fingers curling within his. He smiled. Jake began to smile too.

'Do you like football?' Jake piped up hopefully.

'Never miss a match,' Christien lied without hesitation.

Feeling excluded for the first time since her son had

been born, Tabby watched in a daze as Jake and Christien proceeded to demonstrate that the gap between three years and twenty-nine years was not so great as any mere female disinterested in sport might have supposed. But then Christien was bright enough and smooth enough to sell sand in a desert. A bell sounded and she jerked in surprise, only then appreciating that the cottage now possessed a doorbell.

'That will probably be the doctor.' Christien vaulted upright.

'You called out a doctor?' Tabby questioned in some annoyance.

'Don't go, Daddy,' Jake protested worriedly.

Tabby hurried downstairs and opened the door to a suave medic in a suit. Jake clasped in one strong arm, Christien hailed the older man from the top of the stairs, and from that point on, as the French dialogue whizzed back and forth too fast for Tabby to follow and Jake was examined, Christien was in charge. Apart from the occasional question relating to the treatment Jake had received in London for his asthma, Tabby was required to play little part in the discussion that took place.

Finally, having shown the doctor out again, Tabby returned to Jake's bedroom. Christien held a silencing finger to his lips. Her son had fallen asleep in his father's arms. That Christien had won Jake's trust so easily shook Tabby. 'Let me tuck him in.'

'I don't think it would be a good idea to risk waking him up again,' Christien asserted.

Tabby was tempted to snatch Jake from Christien's arms and she was ashamed of her own streak of childish possessiveness. 'You can't be comfortable lying there like that.'

'Why not? Are you the only one of us allowed to show parental affection?' Christien queried, smooth as silk, dark golden eyes flaming satiric gold over his son's downbent head. 'I have a lot of time to make up with Jake. I won't miss out on a single opportunity that comes my way. If *he* is comfortable, I will lie here all night and I really don't care how uncomfortable I get or how you feel about that.'

Hot colour flooded her cheeks. He had thrown down a gauntlet but it was not one she was willing to pick up as yet. She was moving in uncharted territory. Christien had accepted that Jake was his without a single word of the protest she had expected or even a demand for further proof. That was good, she told herself. That he should be angry was natural, she told herself in addition. On the surface, Christien might seem to be handling her bombshell very well but, in reality, he had to be in shock too and he needed time to adjust. It would be foolish of her to argue with him before he had even had the chance to think through what being Jake's father would demand from him.

Tabby sat down on the chair by the wall. She wanted to cuddle Jake, reassure herself that he was fine again, but instead Christien had him and she felt constrained. 'There was really no need for you to contact a doctor,' she remarked. 'It was a very mild attack—'

Christien gave her a hard look of challenge, his strong jawline set firm. 'I can afford the very best medical attention and I intend to avail myself of it for my son's benefit. I would like him to see a couple of consultants. I want to be sure that he receives the best possible treatment.'

'Don't you think that you should discuss that first with me?' Tabby was fighting her own resentment over his high-handed attitude with all her might, for she did not want to be unreasonable.

'For three and a half years you have made all the decisions on our son's behalf and I am not impressed by the value of your judgement.'

Tabby set her teeth together. 'You're not being fair.'

'You kept Jake and I apart by denying me all knowledge of his existence. As a result, my son was forced to go without many advantages that I believe he should have enjoyed from birth,' Christien enumerated coldly. 'How can you expect me to think in terms of being fair to you? Were you fair to him?'

'There is more to life than money. Our son has always had love.'

'A very selfish love,' Christien pronounced with lethal derision. 'Both I and my family would have loved him. You have also deprived him of his cultural heritage—'

'What on earth are you talking about?' Tabby was staring fixedly at him but her throat was convulsing with tears held at bay only by will-power.

Christien dealt her a grim appraisal. 'He speaks neither the Breton language nor French. He is the only child born to a proud and ancient line in this generation. He will mean a great deal to my family—'

'Are you so sure of that? Are you sure they'll be pleased to hear that you have an illegitimate son and that his mother is Gerry Burnside's daughter?' Tabby cut in painfully.

'In France, children born outside marriage have the same rights of inheritance as those born within it. My family are more likely to be shocked that I should have a son who only met me today, a son who speaks not one word of our language and who does not know what it is to be a Laroche,' Christien completed with icy conviction.

A chill ran down Tabby's spine and then spread into her tummy to leave her feeling both cold and hollow. Lashes screening her pained and confused gaze from his, she surveyed them both: the man and the little boy with the same distinctive colouring. She watched Christien smooth back Jake's mop of curls and, noticing that his hand was not quite steady, appreciated that he was not as in control as he would have liked her to believe.

'He looks so like you,' she could not help muttering.

'I know.' Christien sent her a blistering look of condemnation. 'How could you do this to us?'

'Christien—'

'No, you listen to me,' he broke in, low and deadly in tone, for he did not need to raise his voice to make her shiver. 'From the hour he was conceived, he deserved the best we both had to give. His needs transcend your wishes and mine. You should have recognised that before he was even born. But now that I am part of his life, you will not be in a position to forget who and what comes first again.'

That sounded threatening. Tabby wanted to argue with him and demand to know exactly what he meant. However, she did recognise that he had voiced sufficient grains of hard truth to give her pause for thought. But, regardless, he was a man and she reckoned that there was no way he could really understand how fearfully hurt and humiliated she had been on the day of that accident enquiry when he had acted as though she had never meant anything to him. He had made her feel about an inch high and fiercely protective of Jake. She had assumed that Christien would have been even more scornful had she announced that she had given birth to their child. After all, he had demonstrated a complete lack of respect or caring towards her, so why would she have credited that he would react with any greater generosity to his young son? But then he had believed she had started seeing another guy and she had to make allowances for that.

When Tabby woke up, she was lying fully dressed on top of her bed with a bedspread pulled over her. After she'd fallen into a doze, Christien must have carried her through to her own room. It was already after nine in the morning and she scrambled out of bed. Jake's tumbled bed was empty, his pyjamas lying on the floor. Frowning, she sped down the stairs and discovered that she was alone in the cottage. Panic tugging at her as she recalled how Christien had accused *her* of being no better than a kidnapper in keeping him and his son apart, she was almost afraid to read the note that she saw lying on the hearth. Christien's abominable scrawl informed her that he had taken Jake out for a drive in the Ferrari. Slowly, she breathed again. What could be more natural than Jake getting a run in his father's boy-toy car? Christien doing something so predictable and male made her feel a little more secure.

It was a beautiful hot sunny day and she took a green sun-dress from the wardrobe and went for a shower. Christien was so angry with her, so bitter. Would he ever get over that? Would he ever look at events from her point of view and appreciate that she had done what she believed was best? Was Jake to be their only link now? Well, at least Christien seemed keen to form a relationship with Jake, she told herself bracingly. Really that was what was most important. But her eyes ached and burned with unshed tears.

When she heard a car outside, she hurried straight to the door and was surprised to see Manette Bonnard walking up her path with a gaily wrapped parcel clasped in one hand. 'I wanted to thank you for your kindness and understanding yesterday. I hope you have no objection but I have brought a small gift for your son,' the older woman said tautly. 'May I talk to you, *mademoiselle*?'

In bewilderment, Tabby tensed and then, with a rather uneasy smile of acquiescence, she invited her visitor in.

'I'm afraid that I concealed my true identity from you yesterday. I was too embarrassed to admit who I was,' the blonde woman confessed in a troubled rush. 'My name is not Manette Bonnard. I lied about that. I am Christien's mother, Matilde Laroche.'

Tabby was betrayed into a startled exclamation.

'I drove over here to spy on you,' Matilde admitted tightly, discomfited colour mantling her cheeks. 'I thought you had no right to be in this house. I thought you had no right to be with my son.'

As Tabby wondered if the older woman was aware that Christien had spent the night with her that weekend that she had first visited her inheritance, never mind passed the night before under the same roof as well, she could no longer look her visitor in the eye. Worst of all, she could not think of a single thing to say to her either.

'Although I knew nothing about you and had never met you, I told myself four years ago that I hated you because…well, because of who you are—'

As Matilde's eyes filled with tears Tabby took her trembling hand into a sympathetic hold. 'I understand…I really *do* understand—'

'I was mad with grief and it twisted me. But perhaps I was also afraid that I was on the brink of losing my son to a young woman when I was least willing to part with him,' Matilde breathed shakily. 'But that is not an excuse. When I saw how very young you were yesterday, I was surprised, but I was shocked when I met your little boy.'

Christien's mother removed a photograph from her bag and extended it. Tabby studied the snap of Christien as a child of about five or six with a fascination she could not hide.

'Jake is the living image of his father,' Matilde commented.

Thinking of the gift that Matilde Laroche had brought and the acceptance of Jake that that telling gesture conveyed, Tabby just smiled. 'Yes, he is.'

'I am so ashamed of the way I have behaved. I felt my punishment when I recognised my grandson, who is a stranger to me,' Matilde admitted with deep regret. 'For how long has Christien known about Jake?'

Tabby winced. 'I'm afraid that I only told him last night.'

'A long time ago, my aunt, Solange, tried to talk to me about you and Christien and how accidents happen and how we must forgive and go on with our lives, but I was too stubborn and full of self-pity to listen.' Matilde Laroche's guilt was etched in her troubled face.

Tabby urged the older woman to sit down.

'Henri always drove very fast,' she confided. 'Far too fast to stop in the event of an accident.'

As the silence stretched Tabby gathered her courage and began talking too. 'That night my father had a dreadful argument with my stepmother over dinner.

She stormed out of the restaurant and caught a taxi back to the farmhouse.'

'So that was why your father's wife wasn't in his car when it crashed.' Slowly, Matilde shook her head. 'I always wondered about that.'

'I'm not making any excuses for Dad but I would like you to know that, until that holiday, I had never seen him drinking to excess,' Tabby said in a quiet voice. 'Dad had remarried very soon after my own mother's death. That summer he was very unhappy. He and my stepmother weren't getting on and I think he turned to alcohol because he realised that his second marriage had been a terrible mistake.'

'Was he happy with your mother?'

'*Very…*' Tabby's eyes watered. 'They were always talking and teasing each other. He went to pieces when she died. I think he rushed into marriage with Lisa because he was lonely and he couldn't cope—'

'I was like that after Henri went,' Matilde muttered unsteadily and she patted Tabby's hand as if in gratitude for her honesty. 'I couldn't cope either, and since then my grief has been my life. When I saw Jake, I understood that life had gone on without me and that I had caused those closest to me a lot of unhappiness that they did not deserve.'

'You really don't mind about Jake, do you?'

Matilde Laroche studied her in amazement. 'Why would I mind? He is a wonderful child and I am overjoyed that he has been born.'

'Christien has taken Jake out this morning,' Tabby revealed.

The older woman stood up. 'I would not like to intrude by being here when they return. But I am sure you have already guessed that, if you are generous enough to allow it, I would be very happy to have the opportunity to become better acquainted with you and my grandson.'

Tabby grinned. 'We'd be happy too.'

'Will you tell my son about what happened yesterday?'

'No. I think it's bad for Christien to know absolutely everything,' Tabby heard herself admitting, before it occurred to her that such facetiousness might not go down well with his parent.

But Matilde's gaze had taken on a surprised but appreciative gleam of answering amusement and she chuckled as she took her leave of Tabby.

As the morning wore on, and there was still no sign of Christien and Jake reappearing, Tabby became more and more jumpy. She told herself that it was a nonsense to imagine that Christien would have taken off with their son just to teach her a hard lesson, but her imagination was lively and her conscience too uneasy to give her peace. It was noon before she heard a car pulling up and she rushed to the door.

Sheathed in black denim jeans that fitted him like a second skin and a trendy shirt, Christien swung out of a scarlet Aston Martin V8 and scooped Jake out of the car seat fixed in the rear. Tabby's jaw dropped. Last seen, her three-year-old son had been the possessor of a cute mop of black curls. Since then he had had a severe run-in with a barber and not a curl was to be seen.

'What have you done to him?' Tabby heard herself yelp accusingly.

Christien angled a look of pure challenge at her. 'I trashed the girlie hairstyle...you might not have noticed but boys aren't wearing pretty curls this season.'

'It looked girlie,' Jake told his mother slowly but carefully, and he even pronounced it just as his father must have done complete with French accent. Her little boy then carefully arranged himself in the exact same posture as his unrepentant father.

'Girlie is in the eye of the beholder,' Tabby remarked.

'Girlie is girlie,' Christien contradicted.

Christien, she understood, was staking possession on his son and ready, even eager, to fight any attempt to suggest that he might have overreached his new parental boundaries. But, grateful for their return and blessed with great tolerance, Tabby was willing to overlook Christien's current aggressive aura for the sake of peace. She surveyed the two males who owned her heart with helpless appreciation. She missed her son's curls but had to admit that the cropped style was much more boyish. Christien? Christien looked irresistibly sexy and fanciable. Her mouth ran dry. Her breathing quickened. Involuntarily she remembered how she had felt on that sofa and her knees quivered and her face burned with mortification over her own weakness.

'What time did you get up this morning?' Tabby enquired, dredging her attention from him.

'Jake woke up at seven and I took him out for breakfast. Lock up,' Christien urged. 'I want to take you for a drive.'

Tabby did as she was asked and climbed into the passenger seat of the powerful car. 'Where else did you go this morning?'

'Daddy showed me his cars. I got little cars and he's got big cars,' Jake volunteered chirpily.

Jake was already calling Christien Daddy and he said it with such pronounced pride. From the corner of her

eye, Tabby watched Christien's handsome mouth curve
with eloquent satisfaction. Evidently the morning had
been spent in a male bonding session composed of lad-
dish haircuts and car talk. Tabby did not begrudge them
their mutual appreciation. She was delighted that they
had got on so well.

When Christien drove through a colossal and imposing turreted entrance, Tabby tensed and dragged
herself from her preoccupation. 'Where are we?' she
questioned even though she already knew, for at the
end of a very long, arrow-straight drive lined by trees
sat a château.

'We're home!' Jake announced.

'Sorry?' Tabby gasped.

'Duvernay. I needed a change of clothes earlier and
I brought Jake back here before we went out for breakfast,' Christien advanced with the utmost casualness.

She had a delightful image of Christien playing it
cool over breakfast in some café while Jake attempted
to mirror his every action and expression.

'It's very big…' Tabby went on to remark because,
the closer the car got to the ancient building at the end
of the drive, the more enormous the château seemed to
get.

'Where will I sleep?' Jake asked.

'I'll show you later,' his father responded.

Tabby froze at that casual assurance. Christien
brought the car to a halt and sprang out. He lifted out
Jake. A rather rotund lady with a big, friendly smile
was approaching them. Christien introduced Tabby to
Fanchon, who had been his nurse when he was a boy.
Jake planted a confident hand in the older woman's
and, beneath Tabby's disconcerted gaze, woman and
child headed off into the gardens.

'I wanted to speak to you without Jake present,' Christien explained.

Her oval face flushed and set, Tabby came to a halt in the vast marble entrance hall and fixed angry green eyes on Christien. 'Why is my son asking where he is going to sleep? And why did he refer to your home as *his* home?'

'It is a challenge to keep a secret with a chatty three-year-old around.' Christien pressed open a door and stepped back in invitation.

'Well, what I heard was more of a fantasy than a secret!' Tabby retorted sharply, entering a terrifyingly elegant reception room furnished with loads of antiques.

'Is it? Duvernay is where my son belongs.'

Tabby collided with the cold glitter of Christien's challenging appraisal and her tummy gave a frightened lurch. 'At present, our son belongs with me—'

'Long may that arrangement last,' Christien remarked softly, and there was something in his intonation that made goose-bumps rise at the nape of her neck. 'Children need their mothers as much as they need their fathers.'

'Thank you for that vote of confidence.' Tabby tilted her chin but her heart was starting to thump very fast and her chest felt tight. 'Although I have to admit that I haven't a clue why you should take the trouble to tell me that.'

Christien was very still. 'I'm prepared to be generous and make you an offer—'

'I'm not very fussed about the kind of offers you make,' Tabby declared with complete truth.

'Either you hear me out or my lawyers deal with

this situation. Your choice,' Christien traded, smooth as silk.

'We don't have a situation here.' Tabby's hands closed so tight in on themselves that her nails carved dents into her palms. 'I was the one who told you that Jake was your son and you can see him as often as you like. I'm pleased that you want to spend time with him and I can't see why you need to talk about bringing lawyers in.'

'Naturally not. However, I want Jake and you to live with me—'

A disconcerted laugh fell from her dry lips. 'You can't always have what you want—'

'You think not?' A winged ebony brow quirked in open defiance of that statement. Hard dark golden eyes surveyed her. 'If you can't even accept that I have the right to make terms that will enable me to see more of my son, you will leave me with no choice but to challenge you for legal custody.'

This time, Tabby could not have laughed had her life depended on it for she was shattered by that warning assurance.

CHAPTER EIGHT

TABBY imagined trying to fight Christien for custody of Jake and almost winced for she only had love to offer. She struggled to stay calm and make allowances for Christien's anger with her while curiosity prompted her to say, 'What exactly are your terms?'

Christien sent her a slashing smile as if she had already lain down at his feet and awarded him victory. She wanted to slap him so badly that her palm tingled with longing.

'You and Jake move in with me—'

'*Move in?*' Tabby repeated. 'Quantify "moving in" from my point of view.'

'I get to buy you boxes of sexy lingerie and you get all the sex you can handle...as well as a lifestyle most women would envy.'

The tingle in Tabby's palm had become almost unbearable. 'What happens when you get bored?'

'We remain civilised.'

'I'm not civilised. Right now I just want to kill you for having the sheer nerve to suggest I would agree to a casual arrangement of that nature—'

'Even though it is what you want too?' Christien chided. 'Why else did you choose to come to Brittany?'

'I beg your pardon?'

'You could've sold the cottage and never set foot here with our son. Instead you brought him to a property within three kilometres of Duvernay. Your choice of location speaks for itself, *ma belle*.' Christien sent

141

Tabby a knowing look that sent a tide of chagrined colour up into her cheeks at the same time as it made her want to scream at him in a very unladylike fashion. 'It's obvious that you were as eager to see me again as I was to see you—'

'That is untrue!' Tabby slung at him shrilly.

'The first chance you got, you went to bed with me again.'

'Drop dead, Christien.' Tabby stalked past him.

'*Zut alors*...the first chance I got, I went to bed with you too,' Christien drawled. 'Even being furious with you doesn't stop me lusting after you every hour of the day!'

'Every hour?' Tabby queried involuntarily.

'I even dream about you,' he growled.

Tabby concealed the grin that had come at her out of nowhere. If lust was all he could feel, she was happy that it should be a source of hourly torment for him. But on that same thought, the desire to grin ebbed fast. *Was* it possible that she had cherished a subconscious hope that she could be with Christien again in Brittany? Did he know her better than she knew herself?

Whatever, she was in no position to consider an uncommitted relationship with Christien. Everything she did affected Jake and her son was already coping with big changes. In bringing him to France, she had taken him away from all that was familiar. However, she had made the decision to do that with a clear head and the belief that a fresh start would benefit both of them. All right, getting involved with Christien again had been foolish, but at least she could own up to her mistake and guard against repeating it. Jake would be terribly hurt if he got used to his parents being together and they broke up again. He would be damaged by yet another change of home and lifestyle. Their son needed to feel secure.

'Us rushing into a relationship that might turn un-civilised within a few months would be very hard on Jake—'

'I'm sure you'll make a special effort to tell the truth at all times and avoid snogging guys on motorbikes,' Christien murmured with sardonic cool.

'I'd rather be with a bloke who didn't think that *he* was so perfect that it was my job to make all the effort to make things work!' Her green eyes were bright with defiance at his hurtful reminders of her own mistakes, for she was furious that he took no account of his own less than perfect record. 'There's nothing left to dis-cuss, is there? Roll out your lawyers.'

Luxuriant black lashes semi-veiled the simmering golden eyes flaming over her feverishly flushed face. His lithe, well-built body rigid as he reacted to the rebellious challenge she provided, Christien snapped his hands over hers and pulled her close. Bemused by that sudden move in the midst of a serious discussion, Tabby looked up at him in disbelieving bewilderment. 'What do you think you're doing?'

'You need telling, *ma belle*?' Christien chided huskily.

Clamped to his powerful muscular frame, Tabby was insanely aware of the hard male heat of his erection. She knew she ought to push him away but she could not muster the will-power. Hot, melting longing was pooling at the very heart of her. He sank possessive fingers into her caramel-coloured hair and took her soft, ripe mouth by storm. He dragged her down so deep and fast into the passion that she moaned out loud in mingled hunger and fear. She wanted to shimmy down his lean, powerful physique, tantalise him to the edge of desperation and then arrange herself on the nearest horizontal surface like a wanton, willing reward. If anything, the very strength of her need for him scared her enough to make her yank herself back from him.

'*D'accord*...OK,' Christien grated as though the novelty of her new ability to resist him were the equivalent of having a loaded gun put to his head. 'Moving in includes a wedding ring.'

Shock made Tabby blink in slow motion and left her dizzy. 'I don't know much about proposals but I think you ought to have mentioned that about ten minutes sooner. It *was* a proposal of marriage...wasn't it?'

Christien raked brown fingers through his black hair, his molten gaze pinned to her with seething intensity. 'What else?'

Face burning, Tabby endeavoured to dredge her eyes from his riveting dark good looks. Well, at least he wasn't putting up any pretences. Evidently lust was well up to the challenge of getting him to the altar. 'Are you sure about this?'

'If we marry, we'll be providing a proper family environment for Jake...' Christien emerged from a deeply satisfying fantasy of having Tabby on call twenty-four hours a day. He saw her reclining across his gilded four-poster bed upstairs, rushing to Paris for sexy lunch break meetings at his apartment, accompanying him on long, boring business trips to enliven the hours he spent airborne and those spent between the sheets.

Tabby was still in a daze and afraid to believe that he meant what he was saying. 'Yes but—'

'Our son needs both of us.' He would also need a nanny, Christien conceded, permitting a small glimmer of reality to tinge what was fast becoming an erotic daydream.

A wedding ring *would* be a true commitment on his part, Tabby thought. A little glow of happiness started to expand inside her. Why had Christien not made it clear that he was talking about marriage from the outset? Her embryo glow dimmed a little. She had a shrinking suspicion that he might only have come up with the marriage idea as a last resort. A last resort to get her into bed and keep her there until familiarity bred contempt?

Paling, Tabby could not bring herself to meet Christien's eyes. He would be furious, and excusably so, if he knew what she was thinking. At the same time, she found it hard to credit that he was willing to give up his freedom solely for Jake's benefit. And even if he was, it would take more than sex and a praiseworthy wish to be a good parent to hold a marriage together. But then wasn't it also possible that she was misjudging Christien? He might not be in love with her, but that did not mean that he did not have warm feelings for her.

'What about us?' Tabby asked abruptly.

'Us?' Christien looked blank.

'You and me…how you feel about me,' Tabby muttered awkwardly.

Christien vented a husky laugh and treated her to a downright lascivious appraisal that radiated sexual heat. 'Hungry,' he growled without hesitation.

'That's not quite what I meant. When I mentioned how you feel about me…hmm…' Tabby steeled herself to forge ahead and rise above all mortification because it was very clear that he was not about to give her any help.

'What are you getting at?'

'Er…love.' Tabby finally got it out.

Instantly, Christien recoiled. 'What's love got to do with it?'

Tabby's heart sank. Rarely did anyone receive an answer that bristled with such clarity. Talk about slamming the door shut on her dreams! One reference to love and he backed off six feet and could not conceal his revulsion. Even so, he had proposed…after a fashion. Instincts she was ashamed of urged her to accept first, get smart with him about terms later. But he was being so shallow about something that she took very seriously. She wanted her marriage to have the best possible chance of lasting until she was old and grey.

'The civil ceremony will take ten days to organise,' Christien commented.

'I haven't said yes.'

Emanating confidence, Christien bent mocking dark golden eyes on her. 'I'll make the arrangements…now come here.'

Christien began to pull her inch by inch back to him, his hungry gaze devouring her. Tabby breathed in deep. She knew that she was facing a definitive moment in her relationship with Christien. She had never planned anything with him, had never demanded anything from him either. Loving him from the first, she had let her heart rule her head and had then suffered the consequences.

But now Jake had to be considered. Christien himself had stressed that their son's needs should be placed ahead of their own more selfish desires and doubtless that was why he had decided to propose. Unhappily, Tabby could not bring herself to believe that their marriage would last six months on so shallow a basis as sex. If Jake was not to be torn apart by a divorce, Christien would have to be prepared to make more effort.

'Right at this minute, I'm not actually saying yes to marrying you,' Tabby told Christien tautly.

Black brows pleating, Christien jerked back from her again. 'Then what *are* you saying?'

'I'd like to say yes but I just don't think I can. We don't have enough going for us—'

'We have a son and dynamite sexual attraction!'

'If it doesn't work out, it will hurt Jake most of all...a lot of husbands and wives end up hating each other when they split up—'

'Are you always this optimistic?' Christien asked very drily.

'I'm putting Jake first like you said we should.' Tabby thrust up her chin. 'If I did marry you, I know I'd try hard to make it work. But I'm not convinced you would do the same—'

Christien was getting riled. 'Why the hell not?'

'You're spoiled. Life's a breeze for you. You're good-looking, rich and successful and you're just not used to having to make an effort in relationships—'

Christien's stubborn jawline was at an aggressive angle. 'But naturally I *could* make that effort if I had to.'

'Dragging me into the nearest bed wouldn't count,' Tabby returned in some embarrassment, but she knew it needed to be said.

'Since when did I have to drag you?' Christien derided silkily. 'We're talking in circles here, *ma belle.*'

'No, we're not, you're not listening to what I'm saying. I want to marry you, but not if it's likely to end in tears so that Jake suffers for my having made the wrong choice—'

'I can't offer you some miracle guarantee—'

'If you'd loved me, I wouldn't have needed any more.'

'I can make you happy without love,' Christien murmured with immense assurance.

'How far would you be prepared to go to make me happy?' A germ of an idea had occurred to Tabby.

'I'm no quitter.'

At least, she consoled herself, in the radius of his father's unquestioning confidence Jake was highly unlikely to suffer from low self-esteem.

'You said it would be ten days before we can get married. So you've got that amount of time to persuade me that I should marry you—'

'Persuade?' Christien frowned. 'I don't follow.'

'You've got from now until the ceremony to convince me...while we occupy separate beds,' Tabby hastened to add.

The silence pulsed like a live thing.

Christien angled a sardonic scrutiny over her. 'This is a joke...right?'

Tabby stiffened. 'No, it's not a joke. You see, we've never had a normal relationship—'

'"Normal" is defined by separate beds?'

'The very fact that that is the first thing you home in on proves that—'

'I'm a guy and honest enough to admit that separate beds have zero appeal?' Christien slotted in darkly.

'I'd just like us to spend time together, go out to dinner and stuff...I've never had that.' Tabby compressed her lips on that grudging admission. 'Not with anyone. Before I met you, I went around with a crowd but it wasn't really dating and then I fell pregnant.'

Christien had gone very still. 'What about after Jake was born?'

Dully amused at how little he understood about how much parenthood had changed her life, Tabby released a rueful laugh. 'Single mothers aren't high on the hot list of babes in the eyes of male students. I didn't have time to date anyway. I was studying, looking after Jake and working several nights a week to bring in some cash.'

Without the smallest warning, Christien was feeling gutted by guilt and a reluctant awareness of the privileged existence that he took quite for granted. He could easily imagine how he would have felt being saddled with the care of a baby as a teenager and he almost shuddered. She had had to be responsible way beyond her years. Jake's conception had deprived her of all freedom and fun. That she had still got through college was a tribute to her.

'Don't think that I didn't get asked out, because I *was* asked!' Tabby wanted him to know that.

'So why didn't you go?'

Tabby grimaced. 'Blokes tend to assume you're a sure thing if you already have a baby. After I got that message, dating seemed more trouble than it was worth.'

His lean, strong face was taut. 'You don't have to answer this...but have you ever been with anyone but me?'

Glancing up in surprise, Tabby collided with his intent gaze and blushed to the roots of her hair before uttering a sheepish negative.

Something in his chest tightened and he dragged in a deep, ragged breath. He swung away. His son had been as good as a chastity belt. He was ashamed that he was pleased that she had never been to bed with any other guy. After all, self-evidently, he had wrecked her life at seventeen. Ironically that had been the one and only time that he had ever chosen to rely on a lover to take precautions. Why? In certain situations condoms were inconvenient and he had thought of his pleasure rather than her protection.

'D'accord...' Christien squared his wide shoulders like a male ready to assume an unpleasant duty. 'So I demonstrate that I can make you happy without sex...I hope you're not expecting me to be happy too.'

'You might be surprised.'

'Not that surprised,' Christien drawled.

They lunched with Jake at a polished table in a grand dining room lined by rather gloomy ancestral portraits. Even so, she did recognise that the men were a pretty fanciable bunch. After the meal, he informed her that they were flying to Paris.

'Don't be annoyed with me...Jake has an appointment with a specialist this afternoon,' Christien imparted.

'That was quick.' Tabby had no desire to question anything that might benefit her son's health. 'Money talks—'

'Not in this instance. The specialist concerned is a family friend.'

Her face flamed with embarrassment. They called in at the cottage so that she could pack, for he had suggested they stay the night in the city. Zipping shut the bag, suppressing a groan at the noisy sound of Jake spilling his Lego bricks over the tiled floor, she turned round to see Christien watching her from the bedroom doorway. He looked incredibly tall and dark and lethally attractive. Her mouth ran dry, tummy muscles tightening.

'You're never going to live here,' he commented.

Tabby tried to shrug as though she didn't care either way.

'I always play to win...' he murmured silkily.

Her lashes lowered over her eyes as she evaded the stunning directness of his gaze. A ripple of awareness ran down her spine in the heavy silence. The sexual buzz in the atmosphere was intense and her heart was thumping like mad. She drew in a quivering breath. Her nipples were pushing in stiff little points against the lace of her bra cup and a wave of hot pink washed her face.

She watched his brilliant eyes darken and shimmer. He extended a lean brown hand and she grasped it, let him tug her forward.

'We shouldn't,' she said shakily.

'What's a kiss, *ma belle*?'

Downstairs she could hear Jake making 'vroom-vroom' sounds while he played with his cars. Christien leant down. His breath warmed her cheek. She was so excited she stopped breathing. Without laying a hand on her, he tasted her lips, suckled them, savoured the eagerness with which she opened the moist interior to him. She strained up to him, electrified by the penetrating sweep of his tongue, the greedy ache stirring between her thighs in response.

'Christien...' she whimpered shakily.

'Stop acting like a hussy...this is our first date—'

'*A first date?*' Tabby parroted.

Crhistien frowned. 'You asked me for what you called a normal relationship—'

Tabby was nonplussed. 'I *did*?'

'A request which was in effect a direct challenge for me to redo what I seem to have got very wrong the first time around four years back—'

'It...it *was*?'

Christien laughed. 'So you had better learn how to say no...loud and clear. It takes two to play this game and I need all the help I can get.'

Bemused chagrin warming her face, she dropped the heavy bag at his feet and preceded him downstairs. Her body felt heavy on the outside and tight and achy on the inside. In her mind separate beds had already fallen in stature from being a common-sense precaution to being a rather naive and narrow-minded embargo. It was slowly dawning on her that on that score she had no right to feel superior to him: she might love him but, when it came to the lust factor, she was as guilty as he was.

CHAPTER NINE

TABBY and Christien went to Paris with the nursemaid, Fanchon, in tow. The specialist, an expert in the field of childhood asthma, gave Jake a brief examination and booked him in for tests the following day.

Christien owned a seventeenth century town house on Ile St-Louis. It had an incredible location on a picturesque tree-lined quay overlooking the Seine. Admitting that he had several calls to return, he left her to dress for dinner in a guest room. She put on a slender white dress with a plaited brown leather belt that hung low on her hips, and when she tucked their son into bed he wished her goodnight in careful French.

Sleek and handsome in a designer suit, Christien came forward to greet her when she walked into the imposing drawing room. A portly older man stood smiling beside the trays of glorious rings spread out in front of the windows to catch the best light.

Christien curved a light arm to her spine. 'I want you to choose your engagement ring.'

'Wow...you're being so conventional,' she mumbled to cover her delight and surprise with a little cool.

'Maybe it's *too* conventional... If you prefer we can scrap the ring idea,' Christien countered very seriously.

'Don't be daft...I was only teasing.' Having registered that facetious comments could get her into trouble, she hastened over to the rings and fell madly in love with a diamond in a wonderful art deco setting.

'Take your time,' Christien censured, distrusting impulses.

'No, this is it...this is the one,' she insisted. 'It's my favourite era.'

He took her to an exclusive restaurant for dinner.

'This is how it should have been the first night...I should have waited,' Christien conceded. 'But I couldn't keep my hands off you—'

'Let's not talk about stuff like that.' Tabby was getting short of breath just looking across the table at his lean dark features and the aura of sexy confidence he exuded.

'I want to marry you,' Christien said harshly. 'I really *do* want to marry you.'

'But I don't want it to be just because of Jake or...' But she bit back the word 'sex' for suddenly she could see how unfair she was being. He didn't love her, but she was pushing as if she thought pressure might somehow change that and, of course, it wouldn't. If lust and his son were all she had to hold him, maybe she was just going to have to come down to earth and get used to that reality.

She scarcely knew what she ate at that meal. She saw other women glancing at him, admiring that hard bronzed profile, the grace of the lean hands he used to express himself while he talked. An intensity of love that was almost terrifying filled her.

'Shall we go to a club?' he asked over coffee.

'Not in the mood.' She didn't trust herself to look at him in the cab. She wanted him. She wanted him so badly it hurt to say no to herself. He followed her into Jake's room. From the floor he retrieved the worn white stuffed lamb that Jake had slept with since he was a baby. He slotted it in beside their son and straightened his bedding.

'*Bon Dieu*…I can't believe he's ours,' Christien confided huskily. 'When I think about him or look at him I have that same sense of wonder I used to have as a child at *Noël*…at Christmas.'

Her eyes prickled. 'Thank goodness…I thought it was only me who could get soppy about him.'

In the corridor, Christien paused, lean, powerful face taut. 'If I had known you were carrying my baby, I would have been there for you,' he asserted in a driven undertone. 'But that day at the accident enquiry, I didn't trust myself to be alone with you—'

'But why?' she whispered, breaking into that emotive flood.

'I was angry as hell. I believed that you'd two-timed me with the biker. I'd let that conviction destroy even the good memories I had of you,' he admitted grimly. 'I was still very bitter. I didn't want you to know what I was feeling.'

He had freed her from the fear that he had rejected her that day because she was Gerry Burnside's daughter. She knew how strong his pride was, but he had told her more than he probably realised. All those months later, he had still been furious and bitter over her supposed betrayal. The longevity of those emotions suggested to her that she had meant something rather more to Christien Laroche than a casual summer lover.

'But I can see that you thought I was cruel. That was never my intention. I didn't appreciate that I had the power to hurt you that day,' Christien completed.

She stretched up on tiptoes, linked her arms round his neck and raised shining eyes to his. 'I know. Thank you for my gorgeous ring.'

With infuriating control, Christien set her back from him again. 'We have an early start tomorrow.'

It was a warm night and she wasn't in the mood to go to bed. Earlier in the evening, Christien had given her a tour of the apartment and there was a pool in the basement. She descended the stairs and used the atmospheric lighting to illuminate the glorious pool shaped like a lake. Never had she seen a stretch of water look quite so enticing.

Stripping where she stood, she padded down the Roman steps and sighed with appreciation as the cool, silky water washed her overheated skin. She swam a length and then let her eyes drift shut while she floated.

'You'd better vacate the water if you don't want to be ravished,' Christien's husky drawl warned.

Her eyes flew wide and she flipped over with an ungainly splash. He was hunkered down by the side of the pool, bronzed hair-roughened chest bare. He vaulted upright again.

'This is my equivalent of a cold shower,' he told her bluntly. 'You're looking at a guy on the edge, *mon ange.*'

Her face suffused with colour as she noticed the bulge of male arousal delineated by the tight black denim. He unsnapped the waistband, undid the zip with obvious difficulty. Again she noticed the silky furrow of black hair that ran down over his flat, taut stomach. Dragging her half-embarrassed, half-appreciative attention from him, she swam for the steps. Only as she emerged from the water did she appreciate her own nudity and how provocative it must seem to Christien that she had not even set out a towel with which to cover herself.

Christien was stopped in his tracks by the sight of

her. Her hair was a thick, damp tangle round her animated face and her skin had the luscious glow of a sun-ripened peach.

'I swear I didn't know you were coming down here,' Tabby muttered feverishly. 'I swear it.'

'Stand up...drop your hands...show me what I want to see.' Christien's rich dark accented drawl was bold and rough-edged.

She met burning golden eyes and her heartbeat quickened and her head swam. She arched her spine, let her hands fall to her side, listened to the indrawn hiss of his breath with an inner stab of feminine satisfaction. 'It's our first date,' she reminded him.

'So I'm a sure thing, *ma belle*.' His gaze clung to the creamy swell of her voluptuous breasts and lingered on distended pink nipples still beaded with water. A groan broke low in his throat. 'In fact, I'm a pushover...I'm the sort of guy who gives his all on a first date.'

'Are you?' Tabby shivered although she was not cold. She was, however, very wound up. She knew she ought to run like hell. He was putting out vibes like placards: go...or else. She had to be a wanton hussy because just the thought of his knowing hands on her left her giddy and weak. Standing there naked in front of him while he looked her over, she felt shameless, but it was very exciting too.

He reached for her in one sudden movement. He took her mouth with sexual savagery, penetrating fast and deep between her lips with an urgency that sent the blood drumming in a crazy beat through her veins. Trembling with desire, she let herself be carried over to the padded bench by the wall. He spread her there and knelt to lick the crystalline water droplets from her breasts and toy with her pointed pink nipples. He tipped her back and spread her thighs to trace the lush, swollen flesh below the soft curls that crowned her womanhood.

As she lay there open to him, her face burned. *'Christien—'*

'You've got shy,' Christien teased with hungry appreciation and he located the tiny bud that was unbearably sensitive and wrenched a startled gasp from her.

Hot, almost painful sensation was tugging at her every sense, making it more and more impossible for her to concentrate on anything but her own pleasure.

'This is one more reason why you have to marry me,' Christien growled with raw satisfaction. 'You're down here at two in the morning because you can't sleep for wanting me and I'm the same. We belong together.'

'But—'

'Don't you dare say "but" to me,' Christien told her bossily. 'You can stuff the separate beds too.'

He slid a finger into the slick heat of her and she was lost. He employed his mouth and the tip of his tongue on her most tender place. Writhing in abandonment, she moaned like a soul in torment and clutched at his hair. Pleasure as she had never known had her in its grip and she couldn't speak, couldn't think, couldn't handle anything but the incredible impact of what he was doing to her. Then, when she was way beyond any form of control, he lifted her up as though she were a doll, turned her over to arrange her exactly to his liking and drove his hard shaft into her tight, wet sheath from behind.

'Oh...*oh!*' Tabby cried out in sensual shock as he held her fast and delved deeper with every sure stroke.

His ruthless domination was indescribably exciting. Setting up a pagan rhythm, he proceeded to drive her out of her mind with excitement. She hit a high in a blinding instant of shattering release and her entire body convulsed in an explosive orgasm. Her legs just collapsed under her at that point. With an understanding laugh, Christien pulled out of her, threw himself down on the bench and lifted her up to bring her back down on top of him.

'I'm so hot for you, I feel like an animal,' he confessed raggedly.

She whimpered as he eased back into her passion-moistened depths.

'Am I being too rough?' he groaned.

'No...I'm passing out with pleasure,' she managed to mumble.

Reassured, he pushed her hair off her damp brow, kissed her and spread her thighs a little more to deepen his penetration with an earthy groan of appreciation. *'Moi aussi, ma belle.'*

The wild pleasure began to build afresh for her. When his magnificent body shuddered with the raw excitement of his own release, he sent her flying to the same uncontrollable heights of fulfilment a second time. It was a burst of ecstasy so intense that her eyes were awash with tears in the aftermath. Clasping him close and glorying in the wondrously familiar scent of his hot, damp masculinity, she knew that she never wanted to let him go.

'We're sleeping together tonight too,' Christien delivered, pressing a kiss to her temples, lacing his fingers into her tumbled hair and then smoothing the tangled tresses again. '*Ciel!* Suppose one of us was to die to-morrow…imagine how we would feel if we had slept apart.'

That very suggestion was too much for Tabby in the emotional mood she was in and she sobbed, 'Don't ever say anything like that!'

'I was only kidding.' Christien hugged her so tight that breathing was an impossibility. For a sickening second he had been jarred by the thought of how he would have felt had she been in that car with her father and his friends that night almost four years earlier, and it was as if he had been punched in the gut by a iron fist.

'But stuff like that happens—'

'We've already come through a lifetime of bad luck and we're together again,' Christien drawled forcefully, but he was wondering uneasily what was the matter with him.

Why was he talking and thinking the way he was? It was weird. He felt decidedly queasy about the amount of unfamiliar emotion assailing him, never mind his own imaginative flight of folly that had caused her to burst into tears in the first instance. Of course, he was fond of her. Naturally. There was nothing wrong with affection, was there? She lapped up stuff like that too, he reminded himself, relaxing again. The hugs, the hand holding, the cards, the flowers, all the stupid, meaningless mush. He hugged her, held her hand and resolved to have flowers sent to her in the morning. He was really only catering to *her* needs and only a miserable, selfish bastard would withhold the little touches that made her content.

He carried Tabby into a big walk-in shower. 'By day

you can be as proper as a Victorian virgin but at night, you're mine,' he told her.

Her body had a sweet, lingering ache of satisfaction that filled her with languor. A towel wrapped round her in a sarong, he took her back up to his room. There he unwrapped her again with the care of a male performing a symbolic act and slid her beneath the sheet. Shedding his jeans, he climbed in beside her and hauled her close. Love spread through Tabby in a warm wave of security. Nestling into him, charmed by the fact that he was holding her hand even though it was not really comfortable, she went straight to sleep.

Christien woke to find his three-year-old son staring at him from the foot of the bed.

'What are you doing in Mummy's bed?' Jake asked, wide-eyed.

'She had a nightmare,' Christien responded glibly.

'What happened to her nightie?' Jake demanded.

'It fell off…when she was having the nightmare,' Christien told him boldly, but a faint flush of colour underscored his superb cheekbones.

Tabby, who had woken up too, started to laugh.

'You're supposed to be supporting me here,' Christien breathed in a meaningful undertone out of the corner of his handsome mouth.

'You'll have to do better than that to get support!' Tabby spluttered, for she was in the grip of helpless giggles.

Christien held her until she subsided: Tabby under one arm, their son, who seemed to find giggles highly contagious, beneath the other. Should he call his own mother to tell her that he was marrying Gerry Burnside's daughter? He was no coward, but he felt more like sending a note and keeping his distance until the hysterics were over and the tears had dried. Phoning, he decided, would be the safest and kindest first line of approach. Did he then risk taking Tabby for a brief visit? For perhaps ten minutes? He refused to contemplate the possibility of Tabby being slighted or hurt. Ought he to say something to that effect to his mother beforehand? Above Tabby's vulnerable head, he grimaced and his possessive embrace became even more pronounced.

That afternoon, Christien shepherded Tabby and Jake into his mother's apartment. It seemed less gloomy than it had been on his last visit. The curtains were no longer half shut and some of the blinds that blocked the sunlight had been raised. He could only stare when his parent walked to greet them, looking quite unrecognisable, not only because she had a tentative smile on her face, but also because she was wearing something other than black for the first time in almost four years: a dark blue dress.

'*Madame…*' Tabby murmured cheerfully, offering her cheek French-fashion for his elegant mother's salutation.

'Tabby…' Christien's parent murmured in warm welcome, kissing her on both cheeks. 'Please call me Matilde.'

Jake opened his arms for a hug. Matilde knelt down to oblige and informed the little boy that the French word for grandmother was *mamie*.

Christien could not credit what he was seeing. It was picture perfect. It seemed too good to be true that the very first time his parent laid eyes on Tabby, she should greet the younger woman like a cherished family member. But there it was: his mother was enthusing over

Tabby's engagement ring and listening to Jake's chatter while their son hung onto the older woman's hand.

Christien cleared his throat. Both women gave him an innocent look of enquiry.

'*Non*...the show is over,' Christien pronounced drily. 'I'm not fooled. I'm not that stupid. The two of you have met before!'

'How did you know?' Tabby demanded in exasperation.

A rerun of Veronique's first meeting with his parent after their engagement had replayed in Christien's memory. Although she'd known the brunette since childhood, his mother's polite reception of her future daughter-in-law had had little warmth. A belated deduction that came as a sincere shock to Christien led him into a rare indiscretion.

Christien studied Matilde in surprise. 'You didn't like Veronique...'

The older woman was taken aback by his lack of tact in referring to his former fiancée on such an occasion and then she sighed in answer. 'Even when that young woman was a little girl, I thought she was sly.'

'So how did you meet Tabby?' Christien asked, only casually wondering why Veronique had such a very bad track record when it came to befriending her own sex. Sly?

'Ask us no questions and we will tell you no lies,' Tabby interposed at an instant when, ironically, she was gasping to ask a curious question on her own account. Veronique? Had Christien and his parent been referring to the same woman whom she had met in the Dordogne?

Matilde announced that she wanted to throw a party to celebrate their engagement. As a distraction it was very successful, particularly as Christien was also caught up in silencing his son's innocent attempt to tell Matilde that Tabby had had such a bad nightmare that her nightie had fallen off.

Having left Matilde's apartment, Tabby and Christien were in the lift before Tabby had the opportunity to say, 'Veronique...was that the same Veronique I met years back?'

Christien gave her an uncommunicative nod of confirmation.

So he *had* been seeing the other woman. Tabby almost winced. She was disappointed in him. All right, Veronique had been beautiful and stylish and clever, but she had also been a cold, nasty piece of work as Tabby had found out to her cost after that car crash when she had gone up to the villa in the hope of seeing Christien again. But there it was, deserved or otherwise, evidently Veronique had finally got what she had wanted all along: her chance to shine with Christien as something other than a good mate. For once, however, life appeared to have handed out its just deserts for Christien had obviously been less than impressed, Tabby reflected with a satisfaction that was only human.

But that satisfaction was just as swiftly replaced by a disconcerting stab of unease that prompted her to say, 'I gather that you and Veronique were together a while back...so I don't have anything to do with you breaking up with her, do I?'

'*Ne fais pas l'idiote*...don't be silly!' Telling all, Christien had decided, would only cause distress. In fact it was a kindness to keep quiet for Tabby was happy and an awareness of how recently he had been engaged to Veronique would only make her very *un-happy*...

On the night of their engagement party, Tabby twirled in front of a giant gilt-edged mirror in the grand salon at Duvernay and then twirled again for good measure.

Courtesy of Christien's generosity, an antique Cartier diamond necklace of deco vintage encircled her throat. It looked fabulous and her dress had a to-die-for glamour that thrilled her. Ruby-red in colour, it bared her shoulders, hugged her shapely figure to perfection and fell into a flirty hem round her ankles, scoring on all three counts of being feminine and sexy and chic into the bargain. But without Matilde, she would never have had the nerve to enter the high fashion emporium on the Rue St-Honore where she had found the gown.

The past eight days had been hugely enjoyable for Tabby and jam-packed with activity and entertainment. With Christien she had picnicked below the chestnut trees in the Jardin des Tuileries, visited Disneyland Paris with Jake, toured fabulous art collections and on one memorable occasion had gone out clubbing until dawn. They had talked about her career as an artist and stolen hungry kisses behind doors like guilty teenagers. They had spent virtually every daylight hour together with Christien making up business hours most evenings and Tabby was now fully convinced that she had had very good taste when she'd fallen in love with him almost four years earlier.

He had become so romantic since then too, she thought blissfully. He kept on sending her flowers and buying her little gifts, like the teddy bear with the silly smile that he had said reminded him of her...and big gifts like the diamond necklace and a gorgeous deco bronze of a dancing woman. With Matilde Laroche being so welcoming, Tabby truly felt as though she was becoming part of a family again and that it should be Christien's family was a source of real joy to her for it healed the wounds of the past.

In between times, and regardless of the reality that she had yet to officially give her agreement to marrying Christien, their wedding plans had marched on with Matilde in enthusiastic charge. Tabby's actual spoken agreement had come to seem quite unnecessary. In just thirty-six hours, they would undergo a civil ceremony in the *mairie* or town hall, and that would be followed by a church blessing.

Tabby could hardly wait for the wedding, not least because she and Christien would finally be able to make love again. They had both learned an embarrassing lesson by letting Jake catch them in the same bed before she had a wedding ring on her finger. Not the least of their punishments had been Jake's earnest suggestion that he keep his mother company at night in case she had another nightmare. Indeed Tabby and Christien had reached the conclusion that it was their duty to set their son an example until that magical moment when they could freely point out that married people slept in the same bed.

Christien appeared in the doorway, a sleek and spectacular masculine vision in an Armani evening suit.

'Show-stopping,' he pronounced with intense appreciation when he saw her in the ruby-red dress. 'You look hot and you're mine, *ma belle*.'

The party took off like an express train and the best champagne flowed like a river in flood. Jake got a little over-excited at all the attention he was receiving and had to be reprimanded once or twice. Christien's relatives were generally very much in the older age group and Tabby found them old-fashioned and formal but kindly and inclined to treat her son like a little prince in waiting. Christien had invited only a handful of close friends to the engagement celebration because it was being staged so close to the wedding. Tabby had only contrived to invite one guest of her own: Sean Wendell. Her aunt and her boyfriend were flying in just for the wedding before they travelled on to Australia but unfortunately Tabby's friend, Pippa, was unable to leave her father to manage on his own.

Veronique Giraud staged her entrance when the party was in full swing. Tabby noticed the sudden silence that fell and she glanced up. She was dismayed by the other woman's arrival for she had had no idea that the brunette had been invited. Sporting a stunning black and white evening gown, Veronique headed direct for Christien. As she crossed the floor she performed a couple of fluid teasing steps to the music and extended her hand to Christien. Striding to meet her, he accepted her invitation.

Tabby knew how to jive but had never learned how to do anything else. She had ignored Christien's effort to persuade her that she could easily learn the steps because she had not wanted to risk making a fool of herself at their engagement party. The sight of Veronique smiling while she gracefully circled the floor in Christien's arms sent a shard of angry envy and hurt darting through Tabby.

Indeed, just watching Veronique Tabby could feel herself regressing to the intimidated teenager she had been almost four years earlier. On the day that she was to fly back home with her widowed stepmother, she had hurried up to the Laroche villa to make a desperate last ditch attempt to see Christien before she had to leave France. After all, he had not called her, nor had he been answering his phone.

Veronique had come to the door in the wake of the manservant. 'What do you want?' she demanded rudely.

Tabby was shocked for, up until that point, the brunette had always been pleasant. She found herself asking if she could see Christien as if she was asking for Veronique's permission to do so.

'It's over. Isn't it time you accepted that you've been dumped? He doesn't want to see you.' Veronique dealt Tabby's white drawn face and shadowed eyes a scornful scrutiny and her lip curled. 'He thinks he may have to change his mobile number to shake you off!'

At that confirmation that her calls had been received and that the other woman was as aware of that fact as she was of Christien's evident determination to ignore those same calls, Tabby died a thousand deaths inside herself. Already sick with grief over her father's demise and the appalling suffering of her bereaved friends, she was torn apart by the pain of Christien's rejection for she had never needed him more than she needed him then. She turned to leave at that point but Veronique was the kind of female who specialised in kicking her victims even harder when they were already down.

'Surely you didn't believe that Christien Laroche would get serious with a cheap little scrubber like you? Do you believe in Santa Claus as well?' Veronique sneered.

Tabby dragged herself out of the past and back into the present and threw back her slim shoulders. She was not a teenager any longer and in a day and a half she would be Christien's wife. In those circumstances she could afford to overlook the brunette's spiteful nature and be gracious. After all, whether she liked it or not, it looked as though Veronique was still firmly entrenched in the ranks of Christien's friends and would have to be tolerated.

Some of the older guests were leaving and, having bid them goodnight, Christien was hailed by a friend. Tabby left him to it and returned to the ballroom alone. Veronique was coming towards her and Tabby felt pride demanded that she stay still long enough to acknowledge the other woman with a polite smile.

'Oh, *do* let me see the ring Christien gave you!' Veronique exclaimed with mocking insincerity.

'I'm sure you're not really interested,' Tabby said uncomfortably, feeling horribly small and squat when she had to tip her head back to look up at the tall brunette.

'But naturally I'm dying to make a comparison.' The brunette extended a hand on which a large solitaire diamond glittered on her middle finger.

'Sorry...a comparison?' Tabby stared at her in confusion.

'This is the ring I wore when *I* was engaged to Christien. Look closely at it, expect to see it back on my engagement finger again, because when you screw up as a wife he'll divorce you and I'll comfort him,' Veronique forecast.

Tabby was paralysed to the spot. 'When were you engaged to Christien?'

'Right up until a little scrubber came out of nowhere clutching her bastard brat!' the brunette advanced nastily. 'It pays well to be fertile, doesn't it?'

CHAPTER TEN

ALL the colour in Tabby's face had faded away. Giddy with the force of her disturbed emotions, she turned on her heel and walked away from Veronique.

Veronique was lying. Of course, Christien couldn't have been engaged when Tabby had come back into his life. Christien would have said so. Christien was always such a stickler for honesty. There was no way he could have been Veronique's fiancé, no way on earth! Dry-mouthed and trembling, Tabby lifted a glass of champagne off a waiter's tray and downed it in one.

She espied Christien out in the entrance hall and sped out there at the speed of light to catch him on his own before anyone else could intercept him. 'Veronique just showed me her engagement ring—'

Christien vented what sounded like a French swear word. 'I was planning to tell you after the wedding, *ma belle.*'

Tabby studied him in sick disbelief and took a step back from him. 'You mean…it's *true*? You were engaged to her? When did you and her split up?'

'We'll discuss this later in private,' Christien decreed, distrusting the overwrought wobble in Tabby's voice and the furious look of hurt and condemnation in her green eyes.

'When did you break it off with her?' Tabby snapped.

His lean, strong face clenched. 'What I had with Veronique is not relevant to what I have with you.'

'She just called me a scrubber for the second time in my life…and this time, thanks to you, I *deserve* it!' Tabby accused, but her voice was shaking because her heart felt as if it were breaking up inside her.

'Veronique called you a…*what*?' Christien growled in raging disbelief. 'You must have misheard her—'

'Like heck I did. She called me one four years ago as well. Imagine you being so dumb you didn't even realise she was determined to hook you that far back. But as far as I'm concerned now she can have you back…*and* she's welcome to you!' Tabby slung in fierce conclusion before she stalked back into the ballroom.

Dark anger flaring, Christien went to find Veronique.

'I'm sorry, but Tabby is lying to you.' Veronique sighed in sympathy. 'I think she must be feeling jealous and she's made up this nonsense in a silly attempt to destroy our friendship. Don't be too hard on her. Quite naturally, she's feeling insecure.'

His narrowed gaze probed the gleam in her pale blue eyes. *Sly?* His lean, strong face was grim. 'I am satisfied that Tabby is telling me the truth. If you abuse her again or spread gossip about her or our child, I'll sue you through every court in France until you're ruined.'

Veronique had gone white with shock.

'I make a bitter enemy and I will protect her with the last breath in my body.' Christien's intonation was cold as ice. 'Leave my home. You're not welcome here.'

Having submerged herself in the crush of dancers to evade the risk of Christien's pursuit, Tabby emerged at the far side of the floor. She helped herself to another glass of champagne and drank it down in the hope that the alcohol would help her stay smiling until the last guests had departed. At the far end of the room Matilde Laroche was chatting with relatives. The older woman did not deserve the embarrassment of the newly engaged couple having an open fight at the party she had arranged.

Unfortunately, however, reflections that caused Tabby a great deal of pain and humiliation were already bombarding her from all directions. Christien could only have decided to marry her because of Jake. No wonder Veronique hated her guts! Doubtless Matilde had kept quiet about his having been engaged to Veronique because she also believed that Christien should marry her grandson's mother.

Christien found Tabby taking refuge out on the balcony beyond the ballroom and he breathed in deep when she spun away refusing to look at him. 'Veronique wasn't invited this evening and I made the initial mistake of crediting that she had gatecrashed in a spirit of goodwill. But I told her to leave and she's gone and I assure you that she will not trouble you again—'

'Go away...I hate you!' Tabby gulped back the sob threatening her voice.

'Tabby—'

'Did you or did you not sleep with me when you were engaged to another woman?' Tabby demanded shakily.

In the moonlight, Christien almost groaned out loud.

'You lying, cheating...when I think of the grief you gave me when I lied about my age four years ago and here *you* are...' Words failed Tabby in her angry distress and she stalked past him.

A lean hand snapped round her elbow. 'Don't do

this to us. Just let it go. I remained silent about
Veronique because I didn't want to wreck things—'

Tabby tried to pull free. 'Let go of me!'

'I can't let you walk away in this mood—'

'I'll scream if you don't!'

Christien removed his hand with a flourish. 'This is
insane. You know how it has been between us from
the minute we met again.'

'Lust!' Tabby fired at him in disgust.

Tears were threatening to flood her eyes when she
returned to the ballroom. Sean stopped in front of her.
'What's up? Are you all right?'

'Dance with me,' she begged.

The music was slow and Sean groaned. 'I'm no good
at these ones.'

Tabby wrapped her arms round his neck and mumbled, 'Just shuffle.'

'Have you had a row with Christien?'

'Why would you think that?'

'Oh, no good reason…just he's standing at the edge
of the floor looking furious with both hands clenched
into fists as if I'm making a pass at you,' Sean said.

'Ignore him.'

'He's a big guy and hard to ignore. He is also *very*
jealous. I noticed that the first time I met him. If I let
a single finger stray, he'll haul me off the floor and kill
me, so try not to stumble or do anything that he might
misinterpret.' Sean sighed.

'He's not jealous…why would he be jealous of me?'

'Possibly because he's one of those intense types
who goes overboard when he falls in love—'

'In love?' A sour little laugh fell from Tabby's lips.

'He's been bitten deep by it too. Doesn't like to see
you laughing with another bloke either,' Sean remarked

even more uneasily, holding her back from him at a careful and circumspect distance.

The minute the music paused, Christien strode up and Sean released her with patent relief. Tabby collided with scorching golden eyes and twisted her head away, but Christien was too fast for her and he drew her close.

'I know you're angry with me…but don't start flirting with other guys—'

The champagne was bubbling through her like petrol hitting a bonfire. 'I'll do as I like!'

Christien closed his arms round her. '*Fais ce que je dis*…do as I say. Stay calm—'

'I want to scream at you,' she gasped chokily.

'Scream all you like…just don't flirt. It drives me crazy—'

'How can you act jealous of me after the way you've behaved? When did you get engaged to *her*?' Tabby snapped at him like a bristling cat ready to pounce on prey.

'We should talk about this when you've sober—'

'Are you suggesting I'm drunk?'

'No, I'm doing you the justice of assuming that you only screech when you've had too much champagne,' Christien murmured tautly.

'Answer my question—'

'We got engaged six months ago. It was—'

Tabby lifted her arms and brought them down to break his hold. Frozen-faced and rigid-backed, she walked away. The last hour of the party seemed to fly. Later she could not have said whom she spoke to or what she said, but her cheekbones ached with the smile she kept glued in place. Six months, was all she could think in an agony of jealous hurt. *Six months!*

When the final merrymaker departed, Christien

closed a hand over hers and urged her into the library. She snatched her fingers free of his, folded her arms and finally threw her head high to stare back at him. 'I can't marry you now...'

He lost colour, lean, darkly handsome features setting hard. 'I would have told you about the engagement after the wedding. It wasn't important but I knew that you would regard it in a different light—'

'Your engagement to another woman wasn't important? Wasn't the least you owed her fidelity? And didn't I deserve honesty? Do you think I'd have had anything to do with you if I'd known you belonged to someone else—?'

'*Belong?* What am I? A trophy?' Christien made a sudden angry slashing movement with one brown hand, his frustration unconcealed. 'Last year, Veronique and I talked about how we had got into the habit of using each other as partners on certain social occasions. We were friends and it worked well. We discussed marriage from a practical point of view. I needed a hostess and she valued high social status and a husband who would not interfere in her career, for she is ambitious. We decided that we could have a successful marriage without the emotional entanglements that so often lead to disillusionment—'

'It sounds like one very creepy arrangement to me,' Tabby sniped.

'Fidelity was not required from me. It was not part of our agreement.' Glittering golden eyes sought and held hers, willing her to listen and understand. 'I tell you that only because I don't want you feeling guilty about what happened between us—'

'Veronique told you that you could sleep around?'

Tabby gave him an aghast appraisal. 'And you accepted that? That's disgraceful!'

'Not in her opinion. Veronique does not attach importance to such matters.'

'Well, it's just as well that I'm not marrying you, because if you played away on *me*, I'd make your life hell!' Tabby launched fiercely. 'In fact hell would feel like a four-star paradise by the time I'd finished with you!'

It threw her off balance when Christien seemed to almost smile at that threatening declaration. 'I know,' he acknowledged. 'But tell the average single male that he can have a beautiful, accomplished wife and do as he likes behind closed doors with other women and he'll go for it...until he finds that there's something better—'

'Well, I think it's disgusting!' Tabby spun away.

'But I'm with *you* now—'

Tabby vented a humourless laugh. He was only with her because all Veronique's beauty and accomplishments had proved to be worthless in the face of a three-year-old son in his own handsome image. If Jake had not existed and Tabby had been willing to settle for being a kept woman in that opulent house in the Loire valley, Christien would have stayed engaged to Veronique and he would eventually have married her. She could not forgive him for that. She just could not forgive him for choosing to marry her solely for the benefit of their son. After all, she was not his friend, who inspired his respect and admiration as the brunette did!

There was nothing Christien would not do for Jake. She had seen his relief when the consultant had told them that Jake's asthma was unlikely to get worse and that he looked set to outgrow it. Christien adored his son. He didn't say it, didn't need to say it, just lit up with tender pride and protectiveness around Jake and got down on his knees to play with toy cars as if it were the most fun he had ever had. Her wretched eyes misted over. No, she could not fault him for loving Jake. That would be unfair. But she had a right to her own self-esteem and it was being battered into the ground by the cruel confirmation that the only true interest the guy she loved had in her was her wanton talent for meeting his every passionate demand in bed.

'I'm really sorry that you've been upset by this,' Christien breathed grittily. 'But it doesn't touch us. Can't you see that? I wasn't in love with Veronique and she wasn't in love with me either. I offended her pride by rejecting her. But you and I...we have so much more—'

Her throat ached. 'Yeah...great sex.'

'*Zut alors*...don't talk like that, don't try to talk down what we have.'

'I've never forgotten the way you dumped me four years ago,' she confided tightly. 'You didn't even have the grace to tell me. You let me come up to your family's villa chasing after you—'

His black brows pleated. 'When...when was that?'

'The day I flew back home with my stepmother, Lisa. Veronique met me at the door. I had to face the humiliation of your very good friend telling me I'd been ditched and that you were going to have to change your mobile phone number to shake me off!'

Christien took a hasty step forward and reached for both her hands. 'Veronique had no right. She went behind my back. I never discussed you with her, nor would I have allowed her to speak to you in such a way. But at the time I did believe that you were seeing another guy,' he reminded her. 'I wasn't expecting you to come to the villa—'

'I don't care. You hurt me then…and tonight you hurt and humiliated me again and I can't forgive you…*won't* forgive you!' Tabby's aching eyes were wide to ensure the gathering tears stayed out of sight and she didn't trust herself to listen to his arguments in his own defence. He was downright gorgeous and she loved him, but just then she hated him too. Trailing her fingers free, she yanked the ring off her finger before she could lose her nerve and set it down on the console table beside her.

'No…' Christien grated.

Tabby fled upstairs. She wouldn't let herself cry. She took a nightdress from her bedroom and stole across the corridor to Jake's room where she knew she would not be disturbed. Distressed as she was, she was asleep within minutes of climbing into the twin bed next to her son's. Around dawn she wakened and went for a shower to freshen up. Her head was sore. Too much champagne, just as Christien had said. The night before, she had been all drama and brave defiance. Now in the cold light of day she was trying to imagine what it would do to Jake if the promised wedding failed to take place. He was so excited. And it was not as if Christien were in love with Veronique. But what would it do to her to love Christien without return for years on end? It would humble her, damage her confidence.

The second time she wakened, she was back in her own bed and she sat up in bewilderment. His back turned to her, Christien was lodged by the windows, the curtains partially opened to let the sunlight flood into the elegant room.

'I moved you in here because we have to talk,' he breathed harshly.

'No...I don't know what to say to you—'

Christien swung round. The lines of strain grooved between his nose and mouth were matched by the brooding darkness of his gaze. 'I should have asked you just to listen. I'll do the talking.'

Tabby looped a straying strand of hair off her brow in an effort to hide that she was still reeling from the way events had overtaken them the night before.

'That day four years back, when you tried to see me at the villa and Veronique spoke to you instead, I was probably drunk. After I'd dealt with the formalities of my father's death and my mother shut herself away here demanding to be left alone, I spent the rest of that hideous week drunk.'

Green eyes huge, Tabby gaped at him because he had told her something she would never have suspected for herself, for he always seemed so much in control. 'Perhaps I should've thought of that. Naturally you were having trouble coping—'

Christien dug lean hands into the pockets of his well-cut trousers. 'It was getting by without you I was struggling to handle,' he ground out in a driven undertone.

The silence stretched and stretched.

'*Zut alors*...I was planning to marry you and then I saw you with the biker and it all went pear-shaped on me. When our fathers died in that car accident, I wanted you,' he bit out. 'But pride wouldn't let me have you, so I drank myself into a stupor to ensure I didn't weaken.'

Tabby blinked. She was transfixed. He had been planning to marry her?

Christien shrugged a broad shoulder with something

less than his usual grace. 'I didn't like feeling like that. I watched my mother sink into despair without my father. They had always been very close and for a while after his death she did not want to live without him. It was terrifying to watch. I decided I didn't want to feel like that about any woman *ever*.'

'I can understand that...' Tabby mumbled, and yet she could offer nothing to match his unhappy experience.

Her stepmother had had shallow affections. Aside of a few noisy crying jags, the discovery that she was not as prosperous a widow as she had hoped had infuriated Lisa and ensured that her grief had been even more short-lived.

'Were you serious when you said you were planning to marry me then?' Tabby prompted hesitantly. 'I mean, you were furious with me for lying about my age. How *could* you have been thinking about marrying me?'

'How not?' Clear dark golden eyes met hers in fearless acknowledgement. 'I still wanted you. In the end that's all it came down to.'

Still wanted her but much against his will, she translated. But she was still deep in shock. While being very moody and unsentimental about it, Christien was nonetheless giving her riveting information about what he had felt for her in the past. He was so tense, though, that she felt a sudden shout might shatter him to pieces and she was touched.

Christien expelled his breath in a slow, measured hiss. 'Once you lied to me about your age because you didn't want to lose me. In the same way I chose to hold fire on telling you that I was engaged to

Veronique on terms that you would never understand. Why? *I* didn't want to lose *you.*'

'Didn't you?' Her voice felt all strangled inside her throat.

'That summer we were first together, I was in love with you. What else could it have been? That kind of madness that means you can't bear to be apart for even a few hours?' Christien rested shimmering golden eyes on her. 'I wouldn't admit it to myself but I had never felt for anyone what I felt for you—'

Her nose wrinkled and she made a frantic attempt to fight the tears threatening. 'Oh Christien...' she said thickly.

'When Solange left you the cottage, I used it as an excuse to see you again in London. I had no need to make that a personal visit and I could have made more effort to discourage you from moving to Brittany—'

'But I was *so* determined to make a new life here...I think that you weren't the only one of us hiding from the truth—'

Christien spread graceful brown hands in an inconclusive motion. 'Nothing went to plan then...but then I had no true strategy. Around you, I don't think straight,' he confessed with fierce reluctance. 'I just needed to see you, be with you, make love to you, and that first time I did not even recall that Veronique was a part of my life!'

Tabby scrambled off the bed, crossed the carpet and closed her arms round him tight. She was satisfied for, to her way of thinking, he had not had a normal engagement with the other woman and she could not judge him for his lack of fidelity to a woman who had told him that he might do as he liked.

'But I ended my engagement to Veronique immediately afterwards. I felt guilty but I didn't hesitate,' Christien confirmed.

'*Immediately* afterwards?' It was though yet another weight fell from Tabby's troubled heart, for she needed to know that she could trust him.

'I saw her in Paris and came back to Brittany that evening but you had already left the cottage. Unfortunately something foolish I said out of guilt to Veronique—that I was not thinking of marriage with you—very probably made her even angrier when she learned that I had in fact decided to marry you just as fast as I could.' Christien volunteered with a grimace.

'That's right…at that point you were dreaming of refurbishing the cottage into a delightful residence for a convenient mistress…am I right?'

Beautiful dark golden eyes glinting with wariness, Christien finally nodded.

'You see, I know you…I *know* how your mind works,' Tabby warned him with newly learned assurance. 'The idea of marrying me only came after you found out about Jake and when you realised I wasn't up for the living-in arrangement—'

'Can't you tell when a guy's ready to do anything to get you?'

'Nope…I need it spelt out.' Tabby was hardly breathing as she said it, for she was beginning to believe her wildest dreams had come true without her even appreciating it. It was the way he was looking at her.

Christien scooped her up and sat down on the edge of the bed with her cradled in his arms. 'I love you, *ma belle*. I love you like crazy.'

Tabby heaved an ecstatic sigh. She had not even dared to hope and there he had been sneakily hiding his feelings from her. 'You should have told me that ages ago—'

'It took me a painfully long time to appreciate how I felt—'

Tabby gazed up at him with a dreamy smile. 'I thought it was Jake…I thought you were only marrying me for him—'

'No, he's fantastic, but you are in a class all your own,' Christien confided thickly. 'I want to marry you to make you mine—'

'What do you think I am…some trophy?' Tabby teased.

'My trophy.' Framing her face with not quite steady hands, he tasted her lush mouth with a hungry fervour that threatened to blow her away.

Tabby quivered. 'I love you so much,' she finally told him.

'You *do*?' His charismatic smile flashed out and his beautiful eyes were tender on hers. 'Even though I've screwed up on innumerable occasions?'

'I like it when you screw up—'

'You were supposed to tell me I *don't*…feed my ego,' Christien lamented.

'Your ego is healthy enough—'

'I'm mad for you,' he breathed raggedly.

'We'll be married tomorrow—'

'Tomorrow might as well be a hundred years away. I ache with wanting you—'

'It'll be a very exciting honeymoon,' Tabby promised shamelessly, nestling close to provoke, really loving his desperation.

'We could go for a drive, *mon amour*,' Christien groaned. 'Book into a hotel—'

'No…your mother has me booked into a beauty salon for half of the day as it is—'

'That's stupid…you're gorgeous just the way you are. Don't let them cut your hair.'

Tabby glanced up to see Jake peering round the edge of the door at them.

'Kissy stuff.' Jake pulled a face. 'It's yucky!'

'I think we should start as we mean to go on. Lock the door on him and let your nightie fall off again,' Christien informed her huskily.

'I'm worth waiting for,' Tabby swore with a cheeky smile. She curved into the wonderful reassuring warmth and strength of his big, muscular body and, when Jake hurtled over to join them, gathered Jake in close as well. She was loved. She was loved by both of them, which just made her feel incredible.

Her wedding outfit was a two-piece composed of an embroidered and beaded fitted bodice the same rich green as her eyes and a flowing ivory skirt. An emerald and diamond tiara was anchored to her head, her diamond necklace was at her throat and her wedding present from her groom was the superb diamonds that hung from either ear.

Christien could not take his appreciative gaze from her. He led her up the steps and into the *mairie* for the civil ceremony as though she were a queen. The church blessing followed in the little chapel down the street. Holding hands, they posed for photographs afterwards, her eyes shining, his eyes resting on her with pride and a love he couldn't hide.

The reception was held in the Ritz Hotel in Paris. Alison Davies and her boyfriend looked on in surprise as Tabby took all the luxury and the attention in her

stride. Indeed, the bride's bubbly personality and assurance were much admired and, in her radius, the
groom was less cool than his reputation suggested. His
less discreet relatives hinted that parental opposition
had kept the young couple apart. Their guests began
talking of the match as a 'grande passion'. That Tabby
was penniless and neither stick-thin nor a classic
beauty had been noted. That Christien looked at his
bride as though she were as irresistible as Cleopatra
was also noted. That Tabby had succeeded where the
much-disliked Veronique had failed was sufficient to
ensure that she would become a great social success.

Before leaving the hotel, the bridal couple entrusted
their son, Jake, to the care of his grandmother, Matilde.
A limo whisked them to the airport where they boarded
Christien's private jet for their flight to a honeymoon
hideaway in the Tuscan hills.

Only when the jet was airborne did Christien remove
a letter from his inside pocket. 'This was delivered to
me just before the reception. It's from my great-aunt,
Solange—'

'Solange?' Tabby echoed in disconcertion. 'How
could it be?'

'Solange wrote it the same day that she changed her
will so that you could inherit the cottage. She instructed
the *notaire* that her letter was only to be given to me
in the event of our marriage.'

Tabby was challenged to translate the letter written
in the old lady's spidery handwriting.

Christien came to her rescue. 'In opening, Solange
apologises to me for leaving a part of the Duvernay
estate outside the family—'

'She *does*?' Tabby exclaimed.

'And goes on to congratulate me for marrying you, thereby reuniting the cottage with the estate again—'

'Oh, that's *magic*!' Tabby was tickled pink. 'Obviously you only married me to get the cottage back.'

'Solange concludes by advancing the hope that we enjoy a long and happy life together and states that she always knew we were made for each other.' A rueful charismatic smile curved Christien's handsome mouth. 'She must have guessed even then that I loved you.'

Tabby's eyes stung. 'I wish I had,' she muttered. 'I'd have stormed past Veronique and confronted you that day. You'd have been too drunk to play it cool and you'd have admitted that you had seen Pete kissing me…and we'd have got it all sorted out there and then.'

With a sigh, Christien pulled her into his arms and held her close. 'I was a real smart ass in those days and I was fighting loving you. I'm more mature now—'

'I suppose I was too young to get married then.'

With incredible tenderness, he kissed the sprinkling of tears off her cheeks. 'I adore you. I appreciate you so much more now. Think of all the time we have ahead of us, *ma belle*.'

Her sunny smile began to blossom again and his own slow-burning smile broke out, stunning golden eyes lingering on her with intense appreciation. She found his mouth, dallied there with deliberate provocation, listened to his breathing fracture.

'Make mad, passionate love to me,' she whispered.

'Hussy…' Christien growled adoringly, and he carried her into the sleeping compartment because she was laughing so hard that she could hardly walk.

Your opinion is important to us! Please take a few moments to share your thoughts with us about your experiences with Harlequin and Silhouette books. Your comments will be very useful in ensuring that we deliver books you love to read. *Please take a few minutes to complete the questionnaire, then send it to us at the address below.*

Send your completed questionnaires to:
Harlequin/Silhouette Reader Survey, P.O. Box 9046, Buffalo, NY 14269-9046

1. As you may know, there are many different lines under the Harlequin and Silhouette brands. Each of the lines is listed below. Please check the box that most represents your reading habit for each line.

Line	Currently read this line	Do not read this line	Not sure if I read this line
Harlequin American Romance	❑	❑	❑
Harlequin Duets	❑	❑	❑
Harlequin Romance	❑	❑	❑
Harlequin Historicals	❑	❑	❑
Harlequin Superromance	❑	❑	❑
Harlequin Intrigue	❑	❑	❑
Harlequin Presents	❑	❑	❑
Harlequin Temptation	❑	❑	❑
Harlequin Blaze	❑	❑	❑
Silhouette Special Edition	❑	❑	❑
Silhouette Romance	❑	❑	❑
Silhouette Intimate Moments	❑	❑	❑
Silhouette Desire	❑	❑	❑

2. Which of the following best describes why you bought *this book?* One answer only, please.

the picture on the cover ❑	the title ❑
the author ❑	the line is one I read often ❑
part of a miniseries ❑	saw an ad in another book ❑
saw an ad in a magazine/newsletter ❑	a friend told me about it ❑
I borrowed/was given this book ❑	other: _____ ❑

3. Where did you buy *this book?* One answer only, please.

at Barnes & Noble ❑	at a grocery store ❑
at Waldenbooks ❑	at a drugstore ❑
at Borders ❑	on eHarlequin.com Web site ❑
at another bookstore ❑	from another Web site ❑
at Wal-Mart ❑	Harlequin/Silhouette Reader ❑
at Target ❑	Service/through the mail
at Kmart ❑	used books from anywhere ❑
at another department store ❑	I borrowed/was given this ❑
or mass merchandiser	book

4. On average, how many Harlequin and Silhouette books do you buy at one time?

I buy _____ books at one time ❑
I rarely buy a book ❑

MRQ403HP-1A

5. How many times per month do you shop for any *Harlequin and/or Silhouette* books? One answer only, please.

1 or more times a week	❑	a few times per year	❑
1 to 3 times per month	❑	less often than once a year	❑
1 to 2 times every 3 months	❑	never	❑

6. When you think of your ideal heroine, which *one* statement describes her the best? One answer only, please.

She's a woman who is strong-willed	❑	She's a desirable woman	❑
She's a woman who is needed by others	❑	She's a powerful woman	❑
She's a woman who is taken care of	❑	She's a passionate woman	❑
She's an adventurous woman	❑	She's a sensitive woman	❑

7. The following statements describe types or genres of books that you may be interested in reading. Pick *up to 2 types* of books that you are most interested in.

I like to read about truly romantic relationships	❑
I like to read stories that are sexy romances	❑
I like to read romantic comedies	❑
I like to read a romantic mystery/suspense	❑
I like to read about romantic adventures	❑
I like to read romance stories that involve family	❑
I like to read about a romance in times or places that I have never seen	❑
Other: _____	❑

The following questions help us to group your answers with those readers who are similar to you. Your answers will remain confidential.

8. Please record your year of birth below.

19 _____

9. What is your marital status?

single	❑	married	❑	common-law	❑	widowed	❑
divorced/separated	❑						

10. Do you have children 18 years of age or younger currently living at home?

yes ❑   no ❑

11. Which of the following best describes your employment status?

employed full-time or part-time	❑	homemaker	❑	student	❑
retired	❑	unemployed	❑		

12. Do you have access to the Internet from either home or work?

yes ❑   no ❑

13. Have you ever visited eHarlequin.com?

yes ❑   no ❑

14. What state do you live in?

_____

15. Are you a member of Harlequin/Silhouette Reader Service?

yes ❑   Account # _____   no ❑   MRQ403HP-1B

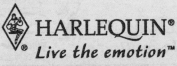

An offer you can't afford to refuse!

High-valued coupons for upcoming books

**A sneak peek at Harlequin's newest line—
Harlequin Flipside™**

**Send away for a hardcover by *New York Times*
bestselling author Debbie Macomber**

How can you get all this?

Buy four Harlequin or Silhouette books during
October–December 2003, fill out the form below and send
the form and four proofs of purchase (cash register receipts)
to the address below.

I accept this amazing offer!
Send me a coupon booklet:

Name (PLEASE PRINT)

Address   Apt. #

City   State/Prov.   Zip/Postal Code

098 KIN DXHT

Please send this form, along with your cash register receipts
as proofs of purchase, to:

In the U.S.:
Harlequin Coupon Booklet Offer, P.O. Box 9071, Buffalo, NY 14269-9071

In Canada:
Harlequin Coupon Booklet Offer, P.O. Box 609, Fort Erie, Ontario L2A 5X3

Allow 4–6 weeks for delivery. Offer expires December 31, 2003.
Offer good only while quantities last.

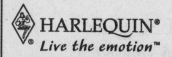

Visit us at www.eHarlequin.com

Q42003